"Are we hav... or a picnic, Hannah?"

Alex asked.

"I always have sessions outside when the weather permits. Being outside makes people more open, less inhibited," Hannah explained, trying not to notice how attractive he looked in his expensive slacks and salmon-colored shirt.

"Let's talk about why you're here," Hannah continued.

I'm here because I want you. Because something about you stimulates me more than anything has in a long time. Wisely, Alex kept these thoughts to himself, but his innocent expression didn't fool Hannah.

"Alex," Hannah began stiffly. "You're my patient and I'm your doctor. Our relationship begins and ends there."

"I understand." He nodded solemnly. Oh yes, he understood very well. She was a woman who wouldn't be rushed. She would need something different than practiced charm and well-rehearsed lines. All he needed to do was figure out what sort of key would work to unlock her defenses, allowing him to gain entry.

Dear Reader,

April . . . the month of showers. Hopefully you'll
have a bridal or baby shower in store for you or a
loved one this month. But if it's only the rainy-day
variety coming your way, don't get the blues, get a
Silhouette Romance novel and sneak back to bed for
a few hours of delightful romantic fantasy!

Silhouette Romance novels always reflect the magic
of love in compelling stories that will make you
laugh and cry. And this month is no exception. Our
heroines find happiness with the heroes of their
dreams—from the boy next door to the handsome,
mysterious stranger. We guarantee their heartwarming
stories will move you time and time again.

April continues our WRITTEN IN THE STARS
series. Each month in 1992 we're proud to present a
book that focuses on the hero and his astrological
sign. This month we're featuring the assertive Aries
man in Carla Cassidy's warm and wonderful
Whatever Alex Wants . . . .

In the months to come, watch for Silhouette
Romance novels by your all-time favorites, including
Diana Palmer, Suzanne Carey, Annette Broadrick,
Brittany Young and many, many more. The
Silhouette Romance authors and editors love to hear
from readers, and we'd love to hear from *you*.

Happy reading!

Valerie Susan Hayward
Senior Editor

CARLA CASSIDY

Whatever Alex Wants...

Silhouette Romance

Published by Silhouette Books New York

America's Publisher of Contemporary Romance

This book is dedicated to my son, who served in Desert
Storm as a paratrooper from the 82nd Airborne Division
of the United States Army. We're proud of you, Frank.

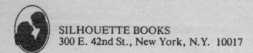

SILHOUETTE BOOKS
300 E. 42nd St., New York, N.Y. 10017

WHATEVER ALEX WANTS...

ISBN: 0-373-08856-6

First Silhouette Books printing April 1992

Books by Carla Cassidy

Silhouette Romance

Patchwork Family #818
Whatever Alex Wants... #856

CARLA CASSIDY

Like most Librans, I am happiest when there is harmony around me, so I often find myself in the role of peacemaker among my friends. *And,* like most Librans, I'll admit to a touch of self-indulgence—give me a bubble bath and a box of chocolates anytime.

With an Aquarian husband, and Leo and Cancer children, our house is full of astrological characteristics that make life interesting—to say the least! But my favorite Libran characteristic—and the one that fits me best—is that of a romantic, which makes it natural to write stories of love and commitment for readers to enjoy.

ARIES

First sign of the Zodiac
March 21 to April 20
Symbol: Ram
Planet: Mars
Element: Fire
Stone: Diamond
Color: Red
Metal: Iron
Flower: Sweet Pea
Lucky Day: Tuesday
Countries: England, Germany, Poland
Cities: Florence, Kracow, Marseilles

Famous Aries

Thomas Jefferson   Bette Davis
Marlon Brando   Diana Ross
Charlie Chaplin   Doris Day

★

Chapter One

Alexander Donaldson III awoke suddenly, unsure exactly as to what had pulled him from his sleep. He lay perfectly still, eyes closed, afraid to disturb the headache he hoped was still soundly sleeping.

Whatever had possessed him to work until the wee hours of the morning, then drive an hour to get home? He should have knocked off a couple of hours earlier instead of trying to accomplish two weeks' work in a single night.

He tensed as he heard a loud thud, recognizing it as the sound that had taken him from his dreams. He opened his eyes, and there, on the other side of the bedroom window that stretched from ceiling to floor level, was a huge woolly white animal with big, curling horns. A sheep—more accurately a ram; it appeared to be quite enamored of its own reflection in the dark-tinted glass.

He knew he should be surprised by the sight, but there was just enough exhaustion left in his system to numb his initial amazement. He watched curiously as the animal lowered his head and butted the window, causing the dull thudding noise that had roused him.

Maybe I'm more tired than I thought, he mused. Maybe I'm hallucinating. After all, what would a sheep be doing here on Long Island? Maybe I'm really still asleep and counting sheep. If that's the case, then the woman who'd just appeared at the window must be Little Bo Peep. No, that couldn't be right, for in every picture he'd ever seen of the nursery-rhyme character, Bo had hair of gold and beautiful, delicate features. The woman now tugging on the sheep was not beautiful, nor was her hair curly blond. Rather, hers was brown and boyishly shorn to fit close to her head. At the moment, her features were twisted in frustration, but from his vantage point they looked ordinary, rather nondescript. As she managed to pull the animal away from his bedroom window and out of his sight, he drifted back to sleep.

Hannah Martinof tugged on the neck of the wool-covered pet like he was a small child and pulled him back toward home.

"Just what do you think you're doing over here? If you're visiting our new neighbor then it's much too early in the morning. If you're running away from home, you should know that the grass is never greener on the other side."

As she and the sheep crested the ridge that separated her land from her neighbor's, and her own place came into view, her heart swelled with pride.

The house was small, having once been the carriage house of a mansion that had burned in the 1920s. The only trace of the original structure was the brick chimney that rose in the middle of the fenced area where Hannah kept her menagerie.

"Come on, Sherman. It's back in the pen for you," she said, leading the sheep back into the fenced enclosure.

"He's a devil, that one."

Hannah looked up and grinned at the gray-haired woman who stood on the front porch with her arms folded across her ample bosom. "He's okay. He just occasionally gets the wanderlust."

"I wish he'd wander his lust right off to Connecticut."

Hannah laughed, knowing how Edna hated the sheep that seemed to take special pleasure in tormenting her. "Where'd you find him this time?" Edna asked, stepping off the front porch and joining Hannah at the fence.

"Up at the big house," Hannah answered, a frown pulling at her features as she thought of the house that had recently appeared over the hill. She'd sat on the ridge day after day for the past month, watching the monstrosity being built. The structure spoiled the last remaining piece of the island's landscape that up to now had escaped overeager developers.

"Did you see anyone?"

Hannah shook her head. "Nobody. But the house looks all ready for occupancy, so it won't be long before we'll have a neighbor."

"Maybe they'll be nice," Edna said softly, placing a hand on Hannah's arm.

"Maybe," Hannah replied, trying to keep an open mind. She'd come to regard this place as her own little paradise, a reward earned for living too long in hell. She couldn't help but feel a little apprehension about sharing this space with strangers—especially strangers who built huge houses that reminded her too sharply of the past she'd thrown away. Like old, spoiled garbage, it had needed to be thrown out.

"Come on. Let's go inside and I'll fix you a nice cup of tea before Carrie arrives for her appointment," suggested Edna, patting Hannah's arm.

Hannah nodded and together the two of them went into the house. The living room was cool and scented with the bouquets of wildflowers that were arranged in jelly jars and bowls all around. The few furnishings were simple: an overstuffed sofa, a matching chair. A miniature rocking chair sat in front of the stone fireplace, inviting a child to sit and enjoy the imaginative shapes a crackling fire provided. At the moment, with spring a passing fancy and summer only a whisper away, the fireplace was cleaned out, the stones washed to their original gray.

"You sit and relax. I'll get the tea," Edna stated.

Hannah complied, knowing it was futile to argue with the older woman, who took her job as Hannah's housekeeper very seriously. Hannah sank down onto the sofa, a smile lifting the corners of her mouth. When she and Edward had divorced, Edward had gotten the house, the car, the paintings, the crystal...everything of monetary value. Hannah had gotten her freedom, the use of this land and Edna... definitely the best end of the deal.

"Here we go," Edna said, reentering the living room with a tray laden with two cups of tea, milk, sugar and sliced lemons. She set the tray down on the coffee table. "So, what are we going to try on Carrie today?"

Hannah smiled at Edna's use of the royal "we." "What do you think of the raccoon?"

Edna considered the suggestion thoughtfully. "No, I think the rabbit would be better. Carrie seems the bunny type to me." Edna clucked her tongue sympathetically. "Poor little dear. Imagine seeing your mother killed like that. It's no wonder she hasn't spoken since the accident—her horror has locked everything inside her." Edna clucked her tongue again.

Hannah's smile faded as she thought of the six-year-old girl who'd witnessed her mother's death in a hit-and-run accident. The child had not spoken a word since the incident nearly two months before. The father had finally sought out Hannah's help, hoping Hannah, with her degree in child psychology and her unorthodox methods, could break the lock that held the child a silent captive.

"Whatever it takes, I'm sure you'll find the way to break through with Carrie. You've been so successful with so many children in the past year," Edna said, as if sensing Hannah's lack of faith in her own abilities.

"I hope so." She sipped her tea thoughtfully. "Even if I get her past this particular crisis, she has a long row to hoe with that father of hers."

"Then you'll just have to give her some survival skills along the way," Edna said in her usual, no-nonsense tone. "After all, you survived not only your father, but Edward." Edna set her teacup back on the tray and stood up. "You go ahead and finish your tea. I'm going to start on lunch."

Hannah nodded absently, her thoughts on Edna's words. *Survived...* yes, that's exactly what she had done. First, a childhood filled with excesses, where her father, a rich and powerful man, had viewed her as just another possession. It had been a childhood where toys and other items had been there before she wished for them, but love was a commodity her father hadn't traded in. Then she'd made the mistake of falling in love with a man who was her father's clone.

Edward Martinof. Handsome, wealthy Edward had promised to love and cherish her, but he'd meant to manipulate and to own. He'd not been abusive with his fists; rather, he'd used his power and money to browbeat her, control her. She'd finally divorced him eight years ago and had emerged feeling worthless and victimized. It wasn't until she had finished her degree in psychology a year ago that she had finally made peace with her past, recognized that the problem had not been in her, but in the men she chose to love. At thirty-three years old, she'd come to the startling conclusion that money breeds power, and power makes victims; she had vowed never to become a victim again.

She pulled herself from her thoughts and finished her cup of tea. She needed to feed the animals before Carrie arrived. They were always more lovable if they'd been fed, and God knew, Carrie needed to feel loved by somebody.

She had just finished feeding the various animals when a long black limousine pulled up the road. The car stirred the dirt as it parked before the house. In a swirl of dust, the chauffeur got out and opened the car's back door. Out stepped little Carrie, looking like a dream child in her designer clothes and with her pale blond hair neatly braided.

Damn him, Hannah thought of the child's father as she hurried toward the little girl, who wore a perpetual expression of bewilderment. Couldn't he have taken the time from his work to bring her himself? Didn't he realize how badly Carrie needed his support right now?

"Hi, Carrie," Hannah said, kneeling down so that she and the child were at eye level. "I'm so glad you've come to visit me again today." It was important that Hannah watch the girl's eyes. As long as Carrie wasn't speaking, the only way Hannah had of communicating with her was by watching her eyes and her body language.

"We're not going inside today," Hannah explained as the uniformed chauffeur got into the car and drove off and Carrie took a tentative step toward the house. "I know the last time you were here we went inside, but I thought it was such a nice day that we'd stay out here and I'll introduce you to my friends." She gestured to the pen.

Carrie made no reply, but her eyes flickered with a hint of interest. Hannah smiled and led the little girl toward the area where the animals were kept. She opened the gate and took Carrie's hand, gratified to feel an answering pressure in the girl's grasp. Good, Carrie was not so deeply withdrawn that she wasn't aware of her surroundings.

"That's Harriet," Hannah said, pointing to the Shetland pony who was munching on the thick green grass. "She loves to give rides to little girls. Maybe sometime when you feel more comfortable, you'll let her give you a ride."

She then guided Carrie to a large tree, and there among the branches was a fat raccoon. "That's Rocky. I found him when he was just a baby. He had a broken leg and once it healed, he liked me so much he decided to stay here." The expression of bewilderment had left Carrie's face and a look of fascination had taken its place. Hannah felt the same sense of satisfaction she always felt when she thought a connection was being made. It never failed. The animals worked magic on the children. There was a special affinity between kids and animals, an affinity Hannah had learned could be healing.

She looked around the fenced enclosure, realizing that one of her menagerie members was conspicuously absent. Sherman had escaped once again. She sighed, knowing she'd have to hunt him down later. In the meantime, her top priority was the wounded child next to her.

She smiled down at Carrie. "Now, over here we have some sweet little bunnies." She led Carrie over to the raised rabbit hutch. "We've got a bunch of bunnies, but there's one special rabbit I want to introduce you to." She opened the hutch door and reached inside. "This is Peter Rabbit," she said, pulling out a large, pure white one. She motioned for Carrie to sit down next to her in the grass. "Peter is a very special rabbit because he loves everyone. He's especially good at keeping secrets. You can tell him anything and he never repeats a word." She stroked the soft fur on the rabbit's back, then looked at Carrie. "Would you like to hold him?"

Carrie seemed to consider the question for a long moment. Finally she nodded her head. Hannah placed the animal in her lap, watching as the little girl scratched gently behind the Peter's floppy ears.

Hannah sat quietly, watching the little girl and the rabbit get acquainted. Trust was something that couldn't be rushed, and Hannah knew that first it would be Peter who would earn Carrie's trust, and only then would Hannah be able to reach the child.

Alex groaned and turned over, his mouth feeling as though he'd been eating dirty socks all night. God, he hated to sleep late; it always made him feel disoriented and gave him a headache. He sat up and grabbed his head to keep it from rolling off his shoulders and hitting the floor.

"Does that groan mean you're ready for coffee?" Jacob Harrison entered the spacious bedroom carrying a tray bearing a cup of coffee and the morning paper.

"Just get a gun and shoot me. Put me out of my misery," Alex replied, releasing his hands slowly from the sides of his head, as if testing to make sure it would stay connected to his neck.

"Then I'd just have to clean up the mess. I much prefer that you try the coffee first," Jacob replied with a droll expression as he placed the tray on the bed across Alex's lap.

Alex grinned at Jacob, trying to coax an answering smile from the elderly, gray-haired man. But Jacob's dignified expression of no-nonsense didn't change. "I should have had you wake me earlier."

"It was nearly morning when you arrived here, sir," Jacob observed.

"There were a lot of things I wanted to finish up at the office before I started my vacation."

"Yes, sir," Jacob replied.

"Thank you, Jacob. I'll be fine now."

Alex watched the old man exit the room. Jacob was as much a part of Alex's life as the board meetings and charity functions he attended. The old man had first worked for Alex's father in the position of valet and chauffeur. When Alex's father had died two years before, along with the wealth, the business holdings and the real estate, Alex had inherited Jacob, who had insisted his place was working for the Donaldson heir in any capacity.

Last week when the builders had completed work on this house and Alex had moved in, he'd installed Jacob as caretaker and general helpmate. The man was invaluable when it came to keeping Alex's sanity intact. Alex had tried many times to get Jacob to loosen up, but the older man had definite ideas on how an employee of Alexander Donaldson III was supposed to act, and he adhered to his own code of maintaining a respectable emotional distance between himself and his employer.

Alex sat up straighter on the bed, opening the newspaper to the financial section. He flipped the pages impatiently until he came to the black-and-white image of himself. He studied the photo for a long moment. It was a good one of him, but exceptionally flattering of Miranda. She would be pleased.

He scanned the article, noting that the reporter had listed all of Alex's accomplishments, attesting to his business acumen. Strange, usually he felt a swelling of self-satisfaction when he saw his business life laid open for public admiration. But this morning there was nothing but a curious disinterest. The same restless disinterest that had colored all his business decisions of late. It was for this reason he'd decided to take a couple of weeks off and get settled in his new house. He'd been driving himself hard, not taking any real time off for the past two years. Besides, if there were any real problems, he was only an hour's car drive away from his Manhattan offices.

He studied the picture of Miranda, noting how the photo downplayed the haughty length of her nose, emphasized her arched eyebrows and the curve of her long neck. Miranda Weatherford. He'd probably eventually marry her. They came from the same background, knew the same people. More than that, it would be a merger of the two families, a joining of power and wealth.

He tossed the paper to the side of the bed and sipped his coffee, staring absently out the window. Had the vision of the sheep and the young woman he'd seen earlier been just that? A vision induced by too little sleep and a brain fogged from overwork? Probably, he conceded, taking another sip of his coffee. He got up out of the bed and walked to the window, smiling at the privacy this seven-acre home afforded him. There was not another house in sight. It was a far different view than he'd had from his East Side town house.

The landscaping company had done a good job. He'd told them that he wanted plenty of trees and flowers, and they had complied. At least a dozen young saplings dotted the immediate area of the backyard, and a circular flower garden had been in full bloom. He frowned. What had happened to the flowers? Yesterday they had been a riot of color—petunias, snapdragons, impatiens, each trying to outdo the other in brilliance and size. However, this morning the flower garden was a monotonous brown, with no hint of a bud or flower in sight. What had happened?

His eyes narrowed as he caught sight of movement in the middle of the garden. As he stared in disbelief, the sheep he'd seen earlier, raised his head, a bedraggled pink petunia hanging from one curly horn.

"Jacob." Alex bellowed. It was one thing to be awakened by a glass-butting sheep. It was quite another to have his expensive landscaping destroyed by the same animal.

"Sir?" Jacob appeared in the doorway, oblivious to the fact that his employer stood naked at the window.

"Who owns that beast?" Alex asked, pointing to the culprit. Jacob approached and peered out.

"I believe it belongs to the woman on the other side of the ridge," Jacob replied. "He seems to have developed a fondness for your flowers." He added the understatement in his usual dry fashion.

"Here." Alex handed Jacob his coffee cup. "This is totally unacceptable and I won't have it. I'll make the owners of the animal understand that I am not cultivating my lawn and garden for the benefit of their sheep." He strode angrily toward the bedroom door.

"Sir?"

Alex paused and turned around impatiently. "What?"

"Might I suggest you dress before you leave?"

"Excellent suggestion, Jacob." Alex flushed, then hurried to dress.

Minutes later, in his little foreign sports car, he drove slowly down the dirt road that led to his nearest neighbor's place. As it came into view he gasped with displeasure. A zoo—he'd built his house right next to a minizoo. His hands clenched tightly on the steering wheel. The real-estate agent had said nothing about this when Alex had bought his property. He parked his car right outside the front of the small house. As he got out, a gray-haired woman stepped onto the front porch, drying her hands on a flowered dish towel.

"Do you own the sheep?" he asked without preamble.

"I most certainly do not," she said, her backbone stiffening defensively. "I just work here. Hannah owns all the animals. Hannah Martinof."

"Where can I find this *Hannah?*" Alex asked, returning the glare the old woman directed at him.

"She's over there beneath those trees. But you can't bother her now. She's..."

Alex turned and strode purposefully toward the small grove of trees near the fenced portion of the yard.

"Hey, you come back here. I said she was busy." The woman left the porch, her short legs hurrying to catch up with him. But Alex was much bigger, much faster, and he reached the shaded area first.

"Are you Hannah?" he asked the woman sitting with a blond-haired child in the tall grass. She looked up at him, startled.

"Hannah, I told him you were busy, but he just came right on out here." The gray-haired woman waved her dish towel at him as if it were a lethal weapon.

"It's all right, Edna," Hannah replied.

Alex paid little attention to their conversation. It was her—the woman who had been at his bedroom window earlier that morning. Bo Peep. Her hair was a shining cap of darkness around her head, just as he'd noticed earlier. But he'd been wrong when he'd thought she wasn't beautiful. Through his window he hadn't noticed that her eyes were green, the exact color of newly printed money, and her skin had the rich luster of a bar of gold. Her features were small and dainty, except for her mouth, which was wide and sensuous.

"He's here about Sherman," Edna said, pulling him from his momentary appraisal.

"Thank you, Edna," Hannah murmured.

Edna turned to leave, but not before directing such a look of scorn at him that Alex felt his toes curl. Terrific...not only did he have a sheep eating all his flowers, he now had an old woman giving him the evil eye. He waited until Edna had walked back toward the house, then turned back to Hannah. His initial surprise at her attractiveness had faded, and anger had returned.

"I understand you own a sheep? A big, woolly, disgusting creature?"

"Could we possible discuss this at another time? I'm rather busy right now." She leaned over and patted the little blond girl on the arm. It was then he noticed that the child held a big white rabbit on her lap.

Alex wasn't accustomed to being placed on hold. Besides, the woman certainly didn't look busy. She was sitting in the shade with a little girl petting a rabbit, for God's sake. "I prefer we discuss it right now."

Hannah looked up at him, recognizing the authority in his voice, an authority she was sure was very rarely denied.

So, this must be my new neighbor, she mused. He was attractive, with dark hair stylishly cut and eyes the color of deep mahogany. Yes, he was attractive, but there was an aggression to his features, a predatory intensity in his dark eyes that instantly made her wary.

He looked familiar, but she couldn't place him and she wondered if she had met him at some time in the past, or if he was merely a symbol of everything she had left behind when she'd made her final break with Edward. In any case, it was obvious he was a man used to wielding power, a man accustomed to having his own way. Well, she certainly was not impressed.

She stood up, carefully smoothing the wrinkles from her ankle-length cotton dress. "Please—" She motioned him to walk with her away from the child. When they had gone a short distance, she turned and glared at him, her green eyes like the waters of a frigid sea. "Obviously you didn't understand. I said that I'm busy. I would appreciate it if you would respect that and come back in an hour. We can discuss my sheep at that time."

"If I wait an hour to talk to you, your sheep will have demolished every flower on my property," he returned.

Hannah flushed. "I apologize for any damage Sherman has done, and I'll be glad to reimburse you, but at the moment I can't do anything. I have a more important commitment here."

"Lady, you have your priorities all mixed-up if you think story hour with your daughter is more important than the destruction of property." There was something about her that was making Alex's anger rise, something in the disdainful look in her eyes as she gazed at him. "I demand you do something about your sheep right now."

Her eyes flashed emerald fire. "Your demands may work very well in your world, but right now you are standing in mine... and that's not all you're standing in."

Alex looked at her blankly for a moment, then as her words penetrated, he gazed down at the ground. He uttered an oath as he realized his Italian loafer was half swallowed by a pile of horse manure.

Chapter Two

"It seems our new neighbor is quite illustrious," Edna observed, the newspaper spread out before her on the kitchen table. "It says here that he and his date were out celebrating his birthday." She frowned. "That makes him an Aries." She said the word as if it were synonymous with ax murderer.

"Yes, I read the article a little while ago," Hannah replied. She got up from the table and poured herself another cup of coffee, her thoughts still on the man who had stormed away earlier in the day. "I really can't say I'm surprised. It was obvious from what little I saw this afternoon that he's aggressive, accustomed to controlling . . . a typical Arian."

"Hmm, I suppose that's why Sherman went over

there, seeking his own kind. The sign of Aries is the ram,'' Edna interjected.

"I suppose,'' Hannah replied. She'd been surprised when Alex hadn't come back after Carrie's appointment. Somehow, even though he hadn't returned, she felt sure she hadn't seen the last of him. It had been her experience that wealthy, powerful men could be very self-righteous when they thought they'd been wronged. And he had been tremendously angry when he'd stalked away. A giggle bubbled to her lips as she thought of him standing in the center of one of Harriet's "surprise packages."

She sat back down at the table across from Edna, pausing a moment to sip her coffee. No wonder he reminded her of Edward—the two men shared the same astrological sign.

"There was something about him that reminded me of Edward,'' Hannah continued thoughtfully. "There was something hard, a hint of ruthlessness in his eyes...." She shivered as a strange bleakness swept over her. "I pity the woman who loses her heart to him. Those kind of men don't know how to love."

"Well, he's a looker, that's for sure,'' Edna commented.

Hannah nodded. Yes, she was willing to concede the fact that Alexander Donaldson was attractive. He'd also radiated a kind of casual arrogance that let her know he was aware of his own attractiveness, confident of his abilities in any arena. He would be a dangerous man to get involved with, one who would demand total acquiescence, complete surrender, but would always hold something of himself back in order to maintain control.

Her thoughts were interrupted by a knock on the front door.

"Sit still," Edna demanded. "It's my job to answer the door."

As she left the kitchen, Hannah smiled. Dear Edna, she had very strong ideas on what her job here as housekeeper entailed, but the line between housekeeper and friend had become increasingly blurred in the passing years.

She looked up as Edna reentered the kitchen, an envelope in hand, a curious expression on her face. "This just came by special messenger. I wonder what it is." Edna held it up to the light, trying to discern what was inside the envelope.

"Why don't I just open it?" Hannah suggested. "Then we'll know."

Edna grinned sheepishly and handed it to her.

Hannah opened the envelope immediately noting the expensive, embossed stationery. As she scanned the contents of the letter, she felt her face grow flush with anger. "The nerve of that man," she said, her teeth clenching around the words. She threw the letter onto the tabletop, watching as Edna picked it up and read it.

The older woman finished reading, the wrinkles in her forehead multiplying as her frown deepened. "This sounds serious."

"It's nothing but a bunch of legal double-talk," Hannah said, scoffing. "It just proves that Alexander Donaldson has the advantage of a lawyer at his fingertips. And this—'' she picked up the letter once again ''—is the way men like Alexander deal with irritations they deem beneath their attention. They pick up the phone and have somebody else handle it.''

"Yes, but, Hannah, we don't need any more trouble, and Sherman did go over to his place and do some damage," Edna reminded her.

Hannah sighed, knowing Edna was right. There had already been two attempts at petitions to get her ousted out of the area. Edward's family had owned this land long before the developers had begun building multimillion-dollar estates and country homes for the rich and famous. Her little house was smack-dab in the center of these newer mansions, and it seemed some of the less friendly neighbors protested her tiny home and crazy menagerie. She only hoped that they wouldn't bother Edward and get him to renege on his promise to let her live here as long as she desired.

"I suppose you're right," she finally conceded. "I don't need to make any more enemies around here, and I am responsible for Sherman's actions. I simply resent the man for running to his lawyer instead of trying to work things out with me personally." She sighed again. "But you're right. I guess I'll walk over there and talk to him."

"You want my whistle?" Edna asked, pulling from beneath her dress the large brass whistle she always wore on a chain around her neck. It was Edna's protection against what she called the "riffraff and perverts" who might want to harm her.

"No, thanks," Hannah replied with a small smile. "I don't fear bodily harm from Alexander Donaldson. I shouldn't be long." She got up from the table and headed out the door.

The sun had nearly disappeared in the west, its last rays painting the sky a pale pink. She walked briskly across the grass that grew wild and untended on her property, her footsteps slowing as she crossed onto the manicured lush lawn of her neighbor.

She'd once believed in the importance of landscaped yards and huge houses filled with elegant furnishings. She'd been raised to believe in this kind of tangible evidence of success. She now realized that for some people, these things were only acquirements obtained to feed a needy soul, sustain a sadly lacking sense of self-worth. She wondered if Alex Donaldson was another of these people, ones who elusively chased some unnameable, unattainable something in an attempt to fill the empty places in his heart.

She scoffed inwardly at these thoughts. Edna called it Hannah's crusading instinct, this need to see that other people attained the same sort of inner peace she had found. However, she was aware that it was presumptuous of her to assume that Alex Donaldson disliked the life-style he was leading.

She groaned as she came to the circular flower bed near the house. "Oh, Sherman," she murmured, seeing that not only had the wayward sheep bitten the heads off of each flower, he had also trampled and uprooted many of them. Despite her personal feelings about men like Alex, she'd have to go in and speak with him, see if she could make amends. She headed around the house to the front door.

Alex shut off his computer and leaned back in the chair, rubbing his temples with the tips of his fingers. He'd spent the past several hours hooked into the main computer terminal in his Manhattan office, conducting business from the office in his home. Despite the fact that he was supposed to be on vacation, Alex was a man accustomed to action, a man addicted to work.

"Sir?" Jacob hesitated at the door, having long ago learned that Alex liked no interruptions when he was working.

"It's all right, Jacob. I'm finished for the night."

"There's a young lady to see you. Ms. Hannah Martinof," Jacob announced.

"Show her into the living room and offer her something to drink. I'll be with her in a moment." Jacob nodded and exited the room, leaving Alex with a thoughtful look on his face. He wasn't surprised she'd come. His lawyer, Tom Richards, could twist words in a letter to make it sound like he was threatening to take away a firstborn child.

Alex felt a tingle of shame sweep over him as he thought of how he'd come back home this afternoon and immediately phoned his lawyer, demanding a threatening letter be written to the woman in question concerning the antics of her pet sheep. He'd overreacted to the whole thing, thanks to his exhaustion. Yes, it had been a ridiculous thing to do, but never in his thirty-six years had Alex felt so utterly ridiculous as when he'd stood there in a pile of horse droppings. His humiliation had fueled his anger, resulting in the call to his lawyer. He'd wanted her to know that Alexander Donaldson III was nobody to laugh at, nobody to take lightly.

He smiled suddenly. Still, she was pretty, although it was not the artificial loveliness he'd come to expect in women. God, those eyes of hers had been luminous and compelling, until they'd spit green fire of anger. It was then that he'd felt the sweet rush of adrenaline flood through him, the same feeling he got when he negotiated a difficult business deal. Challenge...her cool eyes beckoned him, her sensuous lips taunted. She was a hostile company fighting a merger, a hold-out vote that needed careful handling. Something about her called up the high that usually sent him running from deal to deal, acquiring success as easily as banks acquire cash.

He got up from the desk, suddenly anticipating the confrontation with her. Damned if this vacation wasn't suddenly looking quite stimulating, he thought, and went to meet her.

He found her in the living room, perched like an uncomfortable child on the edge of the silk-covered, white sofa. She jumped up suddenly, as if goosed as he entered the room. She looked out of place in the elegant surroundings. "Mr. Donaldson..." she began.

"Alex," he corrected, motioning her to sit down once again. "Would you care for something to drink? I can have Jacob bring us something."

"No, thank you. This isn't exactly a social call." Her eyes flashed a deep, bottle green.

God, she was gorgeous, he thought, sitting down in the chair across from her. She was still clad in the light cotton dress she'd been wearing earlier in the day, and although the dress was loose fitting, it did nothing to hide the curves that lay beneath. And, if her slender ankles were any indication, she had drop-dead gorgeous legs. But it was her face that held his attention. There was a passion there, in the fine bone structure, radiating from her incredible eyes.

For a moment, Alex had the feeling that she was the only thing substantial in the entire room. All the furniture, carefully chosen by his interior decorator to reflect his position and stature, seemed to fade as she captivated his attention completely.

"Mr. Donaldson... Alex?" She looked at him curiously, a trace of caution playing on her features.

"Yes, I assume you're here to discuss your sheep," he answered, rousing himself from mentally cataloging her physical attributes.

"Of course." She flushed, her eyes sparkling with a touch of anger. "I couldn't very well ignore the hand-delivered letter from your esteemed lawyer."

"It must have been a doozy," he said with a small grin.

"I beg your pardon?" She looked at him dumbfounded.

"The letter," he explained. "Tom Richards has always had a way with words. The letter must have been one of his better ones. It *was* effective—it got you here."

"You didn't have to resort to such measures," she retorted. "I told you I would settle the matter with you, but at the time I was busy."

"Right," he said dryly. "I saw how 'busy' you were."

Again her face flushed with color and her eyes flamed with emotion. "For your information, when you came by earlier, I was not indulging in story hour. I was working. That little girl is a patient of mine."

"A patient?" This time it was his turn to look at her dumbfounded. "Are you a doctor?" If she was, then he definitely felt an illness coming on, one that would require a lot of hands-on patient care. He didn't realized he was grinning until she spoke again.

"I'm a psychologist, and I don't see what you find so amusing."

"Nothing," Alex hurriedly assured her, his mind working to digest this new information. So, she was not only beautiful, but intelligent, as well. And prickly as a porcupine. But, somehow this only made her more intriguing to him. He felt the adrenaline flowing once again in his veins, surging at the prospect of challenge. Lately, even his work had failed to rouse in him any excitement, but Hannah Martinof was definitely stimulating a sense of anticipation he hadn't felt for a while. "Martinof?" he said suddenly. "Any relation to Edward Martinof?"

Her face darkened slightly. "I was married to him. We've been divorced for eight years." Something about her expression and her tone of voice let him know that her marriage had not been one of the high points of her life. Little wonder, Alex thought. He'd had business dealings with Edward Martinof and found the man to be a cold, authoritative bastard.

"About the damage Sherman did," she continued. "If you'll have your landscaping company or your gardener replace the ruined flowers and send me the bill, I'll be glad to get it taken care of as soon as possible."

"Don't worry about it. That's not necessary."

She looked at him in surprise. "What do you mean it's not necessary? What about the letter?"

Alex grinned ruefully. "I was very angry when I got back here this afternoon. In my anger, I overreacted and had Tom fire off that letter."

"But I insist," she protested. "I'd like to make up for the damage, the inconvenience."

"I don't think neighbors should be at odds with each other," he said smoothly. "Let's just forget the whole thing. In fact, I was wondering if you'd have dinner with me tomorrow evening." She looked at him as if he'd just asked her to run naked down the middle of Fifth Avenue at high noon.

Hannah stared at him in amazement. Surely he was joking. First, he threatened to sue her; now he was asking her to have dinner with him. Was the man on drugs, or what? "No." She flushed as she realized the answer had shot out of her with all the subtleness of a stick of dynamite blowing up. "I'd much prefer we keep this on a business level. I'll be glad to pay for

Sherman's damage and leave it at that." She lifted her chin a fraction of an inch. "However, I'll be honest with you. My practice is still in its early stages. Depending on the amount of damage to your lawn, I may need to make payments."

"Perhaps I have a solution that would be agreeable to the both of us," he offered.

"What sort of solution?" she asked hesitantly.

"You can counsel me," he said. "Say six counseling sessions in exchange for Sherman's damage."

"Oh, no, I really don't think that's a good idea...."

"It's perfect," he interjected running slipshod over her protests. "I've been meaning to get to a psychologist to work on a little problem, but I never seem to have the time. Now I'm on vacation and I find a psychologist living right next door. It's like fate has thrown us together." He grinned at her, as if tremendously pleased.

Hannah was torn by indecision. Professionally, she felt the pull she always felt when she thought she might be able to help someone. On a personal level, she wondered if the Fates were responsible for this turn of events, somehow having fun at her expense. Still, it was the professional side of her that won out.

"What sort of problem?" she finally asked.

"I have a phobia," he answered without hesitation.

"What sort of phobia?"

"I suffer from arachnophobia."

She stared at him. "You're afraid of eight-legged creatures?" She found it difficult to believe that this man was afraid of anything. Even at ease, he emanated a commanding presence, seemed to be totally in control. "You're afraid of spiders?"

"Terrified," he answered.

Hannah looked at him dubiously. She wasn't sure whether to believe him or not. There was a definite twinkle in his eyes that hinted to her that he wasn't being truthful. Still, this was one way to pay off her debt. "All right," she agreed. "Six sessions."

"How about tomorrow morning, say about nine o'clock for our first session?"

"Ten o'clock," she countered. Although she had nothing going on in the morning, she felt the need to maintain control, establish her own time.

"Fine," he agreed.

Hannah stood up, feeling the overwhelming need to be out of here, away from him. "Then it's all settled. I guess I'll see you in the morning," she said as they walked toward the front door.

"I look forward to it." He opened the door and frowned. "Where's your car?"

"I walked," she answered.

"Well, I can't let you walk home alone in the dark," he replied. "I'll get Jacob to take you home."

"Don't be ridiculous," she returned, fighting down a healthy surge of hostility at his suggestion. It reminded her of the days in her past. How many times in her life had she been relegated to the care of the chauffeur, a housekeeper, a governess? Her entire life had unfolded in the presence of hired help. "I assure you I can get home fine. There's no reason to bother Jacob. Besides, I enjoy walking."

"Then I'll walk with you." He made the announcement in a tone that brooked no argument. Hannah shrugged to prove it didn't matter to her one way or the other. He fell into step beside her.

Neither of them spoke as they walked, leaving the bright area his house lights provided and entering the darkness of the night that existed between their two homes. As they crested the hill, the lights of her place shone like beacons ahead. Like the ever-vigilant lighthouse keeper, Edna had turned on the porch light, illuminating the way for Hannah to get home.

"What made you decide to build your home out here?" she asked, breaking the silence that was making her increasingly uncomfortable. "I know your offices are in New York City."

"I don't know. I guess because I owned this property and I was tired of city living. My family used to spend summer vacations near here, so it was a logical place to choose to build."

"Do you have good memories of your summer vacations?" She had no idea what had prompted the question. She didn't know if it was merely idle curiosity or an interest to discern something personal about him. She sensed, rather than saw the shrug of his broad shoulders at her question.

"The usual, I suppose."

"What's 'the usual'?" she persisted, wondering why she should be concerned with how he spent the lazy summer days of his youth.

"Actually, I don't waste time indulging in memories," he answered.

Hannah nodded, somehow unsurprised by his answer. No, men like Alexander Donaldson didn't waste time on things as unproductive as memories. They were men who worshiped the here and now and tried to predict the future. But never did they allow themselves the pleasure—or pain—of revisiting the past via memories.

"Psychoanalyzing already?" His smile held an easy amusement, but they had walked into the area of light cast by Hannah's house, and she noticed his eyes glittering with a golden-brown cast, like those of a tiger pawing its prey.

"Hannah, is that you?" Edna appeared at the door. "What's he doing here?"

"Alex didn't want me walking home alone since it was dark," Hannah explained.

"Humph." There was enough disbelief in Edna's throat-clearing to suggest that Hannah had just recommended that werewolves make great baby-sitters on the night of a full moon.

"Is she a relative of yours?" Alex asked as the older woman went back into the house.

Hannah smiled, the first real smile he had seen from her, and it was at that moment that Alex consciously decided he wanted her. "No, Edna worked for Edward during my marriage to him. When I divorced him, Edna did the same. She's as close to family as I have.'' She took a step back from Alex, suddenly realizing he was standing much too close. "Good night, and thank you for walking me back.''

She turned abruptly, needing some room to breathe, needing to get away from his overwhelming masculinity. She whirled around so quickly she stumbled onto the first step that led up to the porch. Before she could fall to her knees, his strong arms had caught and steadied her.

His hands held her upper arms, just below where her short sleeves ended. Her flesh was warm beneath his hands, and for a moment Alex fought the impulse to pull her up against him, let her warmth invade his body.

"Thank you," she murmured again, and as he loosened his grip on her arms, she spun away from him and with the speed of an elusive shooting star, she disappeared into the house.

Alex smiled, his hands still tingling from the brief contact with her skin. Yes, there was passion there. It shimmered in her jeweled eyes, it warmed her skin from the inside out.

Arachnophobia. He'd spit out the first thing that had popped into his mind. He'd suddenly realized that if she merely paid for the damage done by her sheep, the check would be in the mail and their paths would probably never pass again. He couldn't let that happen, so he'd invented a phobia for her to cure. He knew he should feel guilty, but he simply couldn't summon that emotion. For him, it had merely been a tool to achieve what he wanted. And he'd decided he wanted Hannah. In fact, he couldn't remember the last time he wanted a woman like he wanted her. She intrigued him, she drew him, she challenged him. Yes, he wanted her, and Alexander Donaldson III always got what he wanted.

Chapter Three

Hannah pulled her bathrobe more closely around her and stepped out onto the front porch. It was early. She'd beaten the sun out of bed. It wasn't rare for her to be up so early. What was rare was for her to feel so unrested due to a night of tossing and turning. And she knew the reason for her restless night. Alex.

She sat down on the wicker chair and took a deep breath of the morning-scented air. Something about Alex had managed to disrupt the peace of mind she'd worked so hard to attain. He'd made her remember things she hadn't wanted to, made her think about dreams she'd long ago cast aside.

When she'd been much younger, she'd dreamed of falling in love with a man who was strong, yet gentle, bold but with a touch of shyness. She'd dreamed of a man aggressive enough to take what he wanted, yet sensitive enough to know when to give.

The problem was, she'd been good at getting the first part of what she wanted. Strong, bold, aggressive. Edward had been all those things. Unfortunately, he hadn't possessed the other qualities to temper the ones he had. The end result had been a marriage that had paralleled her childhood—bleak, lonely and miserable.

She had decided then to steer clear of men who measured everything in life by monetary worth, men whose lives revolved around dollar signs and business deals. Men who were bankrupt in the emotion department.

So, what was it about Alex that had made her toss and turn all night? On the surface he was everything she abhorred.

She sighed, noting the sun was sending hesitant fingers of light over the horizon, as if waving first to see if it was welcome.

"Coffee's on," Edna spoke from the doorway. "Want a cup out here?"

Hannah shook her head. "I'll come inside." She got up and followed Edna into the kitchen. She sat down at the table as Edna poured her some coffee.

"You want to talk about it?" Edna asked, joining her at the table.

"Talk about what?"

"Whatever it is that's making you chew on your bottom lip. You only do it when you have something heavy on your mind."

Hannah realized her lower lip was caught between her teeth, a nervous habit she'd thought she'd outgrown. "I'm preparing myself. I agreed to give Alex six counseling sessions in exchange for Sherman's damage." She waited for Edna's reaction. The older woman didn't disappoint her.

"That's the craziest thing I've ever heard. What does he need counseling for?"

"He says he suffers from arachnophobia."

"Is it contagious?" Edna asked with alarm. Edna boasted she'd never been sick a day of her life, due to the intake of various vitamins each day and a healthy aversion to sick people.

"No, it's not contagious." Hannah laughed. "It means he has a fear of eight-legged creatures, like spiders and scorpions."

"Huh, if you were smart, you'd develop a healthy fear of him. Alexphobia, that's what you need."

"I don't need to develop any such thing," Hannah protested. "I don't intend to get personally involved with him. Our relationship will begin and end with six counseling sessions, and that's it."

"That's what you always say when you start with a patient, but somehow you always manage to get personally involved."

"Well, you don't have to worry about that where Alexander Donaldson is concerned. Personal involvement is the last thing I want from him," Hannah relied with the firmness of her inner conviction.

She was still brimming with that conviction several hours later as she spread out a blanket beneath the same tree where she and Carrie had conducted their session the day before.

As much as she hated to admit it, Edna had been right. For the duration of the therapy, each child she counseled became like her own. She shared their pain as well as their successes. It was this empathy that made her a good psychologist, and that often broke her heart.

Well, she intended to guard her heart closely against the likes of Alex Donaldson. She wasn't about to repeat the mistakes of her past by doing something foolish like falling for a man like him.

She felt both mentally and physically prepared by ten o'clock as she stood on the front porch waiting for his arrival. By ten-fifteen, she was wondering if all her worry had been for nothing. By ten-thirty, she decided he wasn't coming and was just about to fold up the blanket when his little sports car zoomed up the drive, spitting gravel and swirling dust.

"Sorry I'm late," he said, getting out of the car and looking at his wristwatch. "I got hung up with an unexpected phone call. Business." He said the last word as if that explained—and excused—everything.

"Shall we get started?" Hannah motioned him over toward the blanket.

"Are we having a counseling session or a picnic?" He grinned, sitting down cross-legged.

His sense of humor surprised her. She'd seen a flash of it the day before and it had disconcerted her. Again today she found herself surprised, but pleasantly so.

"I always have my sessions outside when the weather permits," she explained, trying not to notice how attractive he looked. Casual elegance was the only way to describe the way he looked in his expensive dress slacks and pale, salmon-colored dress shirt. She particularly liked what the shirt said about him—that he was comfortable, sure of his masculinity and not afraid to wear traditionally feminine colors.

She joined him on the blanket, trying to keep her thoughts carefully schooled to the matter at hand. "It's been my experience that there's something about being outside that makes people more open, less inhibited."

"What about the animals?" he asked, gesturing to the pony, and the sheep who was now tethered by a rope to a portion of the fence. "Are they part of your work or are you just fond of them?"

"They are very much a part of my work," she explained. "Most of the time I work with children. They often find it easy to trust an animal, talk to an animal, rather than deal with adults." She smiled at him, a cool, detached smile. "Do you mind?" She showed him a small, hand-held tape recorder. He shook his head. "Now, enough about my work, let's talk about why you're here."

I'm here because I want you. Because there's something about you that stimulates me more than anything I can remember in a very long time. That was what played in his mind, but wisely he kept these thoughts to himself.

"How long have you been afraid of spiders?"

"For as long as I can remember," he answered, noticing that when she leaned back against the tree, she looked like part of nature herself. Her hair was the same color as the bark of the tree, and her eyes reflected the green of the leaves. She was a wood nymph, promising the warmth of the earth, the fire of the sun. He suddenly realized she was looking at him expectantly as though waiting for an answer to a question. "I'm sorry, what did you say?"

"I asked you if you could recall any specific incident involving spiders."

"No, nothing that I can remember," he said carefully, wondering if he should invent something. He rolled up his shirtsleeves. He wasn't sure whether the heat surrounding him was sun-created or Hannah-generated. But when she gazed at him, her eyes so serious, so full of good intentions, and her lips curved upward in a thoughtful smile, he could swear their surrounding temperature climbed a good ten degrees.

"Tell me, what's the first good memory you have from your childhood?"

"That's easy." He grinned glibly. "The first time my father took me with him to his offices. I must have been about six at the time."

"Why was it good?" She swatted at a honey bee that lazily circled her head.

Yes, get away, bee, he thought. That honey is for me. Sooner or later I want to taste the honey of those lips, feel the sweetness of those curves pressed against me.

"Alex?" Hannah tried to control a sigh of impatience. Trying to get information out of him was like trying to get the last drop out of a catsup bottle. She'd have his attention for a moment, then he seemed to drift off into the ozone. She didn't like the fact that he had rolled up his sleeves, exposing strong forearms covered with dark hair. She didn't like the fact that a small tuft of hair was showing above where his shirt was unbuttoned, making her wonder if it covered his entire chest, or just the area in the middle. "What made that moment in your father's office a good memory?" she repeated.

"I don't know. I guess because for the whole day I had my dad's complete attention." Alex smiled again, running his hand through his hair in an uncharacteristic boyish gesture. "It was great. All the secretaries in the office fawned over me, bringing me sodas and calling me Mr. Donaldson."

Hannah smiled at his obvious pleasure in the memory, then quickly switched tactics. "Now, tell me your first bad memory."

"The day my mother died." The words were out of him before he realized he was even thinking them. The memory, coming so unexpectedly, brought with it a shaft of pain so intense that for a moment it left him breathless. As air returned to his lungs, an irrational anger swept through him. "What the hell does any of this have to do with my being afraid of spiders?"

"Sometimes the reasons for phobias are burrowed in the subconscious. By unleashing other memories, it sometimes calls up the incident that produced the phobia." On impulse, she reached out and captured his hands in hers. His were ice-cold, attesting to the vividness of the memory she had stirred. "I'm sorry if I made you think of something painful."

Alex immediately twisted their hands so that it was he who held hers. "It's no big deal. My mother died when I was nine. It was a black day for me." He shrugged his shoulders as if to dismiss the entire subject. His thumbs moved in little circular motions on the back of her hands. "But I don't mind digging up the memories if it means I get to hold your hands."

Hannah jerked her hands away from his, finding his touch too pleasant, far too sensual. His words raised the defenses she'd felt momentarily lowering. "Alex," she began stiffly. "I agreed to your terms. Six sessions in exchange for the damage to your flower beds. But, if we're going to do this, it must be on my terms. You're my patient. I'm your doctor. Our relationship begins and ends there."

"I understand." He nodded solemnly. Oh, yes, he understood very well. She was a woman who would not be rushed. She would need something different than practiced charm and well-rehearsed lines. All he needed to do was figure out what sort of key would work to unlock her defenses, allow him to gain entry.

"Fine, as long as we understand each other." She smiled, her cool, professional one. "And now, our time is up for today."

Alex looked at her in astonishment. "Already?" He looked at his wristwatch. "But I thought each session was an hour."

"They are," Hannah answered, standing up from the blanket. "Yours was from ten to eleven, and it's eleven."

"But we didn't get started until after ten-thirty," he protested, also rising to his feet.

Hannah saw the frustration on his face and felt a perverse satisfaction in it. "Alex, I was here, ready at ten. You chose to be late."

"I didn't choose to be late," he countered, watching as she began folding up the blanket. "I told you I had a telephone call. It was business." He stressed the last word.

"Which shows me where your priorities lie," she responded. "Business comes before therapy. Tell me, Alex, what else does business come before?"

"What do you mean?"

"If you had a choice, say between a business meeting and a friend's wedding, which would you choose?" She'd thrown down the blanket and faced him, hands on her hips, her eyes lit with the same fire of anger he'd seen the day before. Only this time he had no idea what he had done to provoke it.

"I don't know. It would depend on the importance of the business meeting," he answered honestly.

"If the choice was between business and a romantic liaison, which would be your priority?"

"That's easy." He grinned. "I've always believed in business before pleasure."

"What about a child's birthday party? A once-in-a-lifetime opportunity to see Halley's Comet, a funeral for a close friend or relative? When does business ever take a back seat?" She flushed suddenly. "I'm sorry." She ran a hand though her hair, suddenly looking achingly vulnerable. "I had no right to say those things."

"It's all right."

"No, it isn't all right," she continued. "I'm blaming you for things that have nothing to do with you. I've been fighting off a wave of frustration since yesterday."

"Tell me about it," he prompted, wanting to connect with her, wanting to erase the tense lines that suddenly marred her lovely forehead.

Hannah heaved a deep sigh. "I have a patient right now who I'm really worried about." He nodded and she continued. "She saw her mother killed by a hit-and-run driver and has stopped talking. Her father has immersed himself in his work, dealing with his loss by putting in long hours. He simply doesn't understand that what the child needs most right now is him." She danced her hand through her hair once again and Alex found the gesture most appealing. "It's an endless cycle of unhappiness. Probably her father was raised by parents who had no real personal contact with him, and she in turn will make the same mistake with her children, because she'll know no other way."

"And it's probably a good thing I don't have any children because I'd make the same sort of mistakes?" It was a question, with his dark eyebrows raising quizzically.

"I'm not sure. Perhaps." Hannah bent down and picked up the blanket once again. "Are you planning on having children someday?"

"Who knows?" he answered, shoving his hands in his pockets as he thought of Miranda. Miranda had made it very clear that she was not interested in having children and ruining the svelte shape she worked so hard to maintain.

"Well, again. I apologize. It's a topic that's one of my favorite crusades."

"It simply shows me you're a caring individual." His gaze was warm on her, causing a tingle of heat to rush through her.

"Shall we say tomorrow at nine o'clock for the next session?" she asked, briskly folding up the blanket and picking up the small tape recorder. Her tone also let him know she was dismissing him. Although inwardly he balked, unaccustomed to being dismissed, he decided to leave. Besides, he'd told Tom he would get back to him concerning the terms for a merger deal they were putting together. Telling her goodbye, he jumped into his car and drove toward home.

Hannah watched him go, her expression troubled. It had become quite obvious to her that Alex was on the prowl, and he'd spotted her as his quarry. His gaze had told her he was interested in her not as a doctor, but as a woman. His hands when they had held hers had transmitted the message loud and clear.

Well, she would just have to ignore his not-so-subtle looks and avoid all physical contact with him. She knew herself well enough to know that she was vul-

nerable to Alex's type, and she was realistic enough to
know that he was probably merely looking for a stimulating way to pass his vacation. Well, she wasn't
about to become his vacation toy. She wasn't going to
be his anything.

"They hit us again last night," Edna said in greeting when Hannah stumbled into the kitchen for coffee the next morning.

Hannah groaned and reached for the steaming cup
of coffee Edna offered. "How badly?"

"Red spray paint on all four sides of the shed."

Hannah moaned again. "I don't even want to look
until I've finished this." She sat down at the table and
took a cautious sip of the hot brew.

"Should I call the police?"

Hannah shook her head. "Why? We both know
they can't do anything."

"Or won't," Edna retorted.

"Or won't," Hannah agreed. "I'll take care of the
shed first thing this morning. A few coats of paint always does the trick."

"A good spanking on the seat of some kids' pants
would also solve the problem," Edna said with a dark
expression.

"The kids are only acting out what their parents are
saying."

"Then somebody should spank the parents' back-
sides."

Hannah smiled at Edna's vehemence. "Hopefully, if we just ignore it, they'll get tired and leave us alone."

Edna nodded, reaching behind her to untie the apron that covered her plumpness. "I'm going to the grocery store. Is there anything in particular you're hungry for?"

Yes, a man with dark hair and golden eyes who'll hold me tight through the night. A man who can make me forget all my yesterdays and anticipate each tomorrow.

"Hannah?"

"Oh, no, nothing." Hannah flushed, embarrassed at the direction her thoughts had taken, and the man who'd immediately come to mind.

"I should be back in about an hour," Edna said, grabbing her pocketbook off the counter and smoothing her gray curls with one plump hand.

"And I suppose I'd better get started on that shed," Hannah replied, draining her coffee and standing up.

Minutes after Edna had left, Hannah stepped outside onto the front porch, sighing as she saw the shed where she kept all the feed for the animals. The pristine white of the building had been marred by the heavy-handed use of a can of brilliant red spray paint. On each side was a message: *Get Out. Move Away. Leave Town. Go Now!*

"They aren't very original," she muttered, grabbing cans of white paint and brushes from inside the shed. The messages didn't frighten Hannah, nor did she find them ominous. They were merely an irritation. Stifling another sigh, she set up a ladder, popped open a can of paint and began the task of undoing the damage.

She'd almost finished painting one side when Alex's car pulled up. Glancing at her watch she realized it was exactly nine o'clock, time for his appointment.

"What happened?" He was out of the car and by the shed in an instant, a grim expression on his face.

"It seems we had some nocturnal visitors," Hannah explained, stepping down off the ladder. "And they don't seem to be overly fond of me."

"Have you called the police? Do you know who's responsible?"

"The police won't do anything unless I have positive proof of who's doing it, and I don't. I only have a sneaking suspicion."

"This has happened before?"

She nodded. "Twice before." She smiled apologetically. "Just let me rinse off this brush and we can get started."

"Forget my appointment," he said impatiently. "Do you have another paintbrush?"

"Yes, but..."

"No buts. You can give me another appointment. Right now it's more important that we take care of this mess and while we're working you can tell me why somebody would do this to you." Without waiting for her protest, Alex found another brush and dipped it into the paint. "Now, talk," he demanded, but with a friendly smile that made her forgive the authoritarian tone.

"There's not a lot to tell," Hannah said, climbing back up the ladder as he worked next to her. "A couple of months ago Sherman got loose and visited another new neighbor. He ate some exotic plants they had in their backyard. They were really angry, even though I paid to have the plants replaced. Since then, they've attempted to start petitions to get me and my animals out of the neighborhood."

"And you think they're the ones who did this?"

"Not them, but they have two teenage sons. The first time the shed was painted, Edna saw the two boys in the store and they bragged to her about their artistic talents."

"Did you go to the police then?" he asked, a note of outrage in his voice.

Hannah nodded. "And the police talked to the boys and the boys said Edna was lying. Their parents vouched for the boys, said they were both in the house with them the night the shed was painted."

Alex shook his head as if finding the whole thing unbelievable. "It must be frustrating for you," he observed.

She shrugged her shoulders. "A little, but what they are going to discover is that I can be as stubborn as they can be. They can keep painting the shed, but I'm going to keep repainting, and I'm not going anywhere."

He grinned up at her, admiring not only her tenacity, but also the rounded curve of her derriere presented to him at eye level as she took a step higher up the ladder. He'd been right when he'd guessed she had gorgeous legs. Clad in jean shorts, they were tanned and shapely, tempting a man to distraction.

Alex and Hannah both turned as a car drove up the drive. "That's Edna coming back from the store," Hannah said, turning back to her work.

Alex also continued painting, trying not to focus on the fact that Hannah's scent surrounded him. It was the smell of a cool woodland full of hidden mysteries and dark secrets. He didn't want to focus on how utterly appealing she was because he didn't want to lose control, rush things and end up messing everything up.

"I brought you something cold to drink," Edna announced from behind them, holding out two glasses of iced tea.

"Oh, Edna, you're a lifesaver," Hannah exclaimed, descending the ladder and wiping her gleaming forehead with the back of her hand.

"There's nothing more refreshing than a glass of freshly brewed tea." Alex smiled engagingly at the older woman.

"Humph, it's instant," she replied, and with a glare, thrust the glass in his hand.

"She doesn't like me very much, does she?" Alex mused as Edna stalked back to the house.

"Edna's very protective of me," Hannah answered, drinking deeply of the cold tea.

"Yeah, sort of like a cross between a pit bull and a Nazi soldier," he remarked dryly, causing Hannah to giggle and choke.

"I don't think I'll repeat that to her. It certainly wouldn't help her change her opinion of you," Hannah laughed.

"Why don't you let me up on the ladder for a while?" Alex suggested, thinking that if he had to look up and see her sweetly rounded bottom one more time he was going to lose his mind.

"Alex, I really appreciate all your help, but it's not necessary for you..."

"Do you like to paint sheds?" he asked, a small smile on his face.

"Not particularly," she returned with an answering smile.

"Then I'll help," he said, climbing up the ladder and holding out his hand for the paintbrush. Hannah handed him a brush, warmth flooding through her as he smiled down at her. Then he began painting.

They fell into a companionable silence as they worked. Hannah found herself admiring Alex's physical attributes. For a man who spent much of his time in an office, he certainly had a good physique. Even though his trousers were covering them, she could tell his buttocks were firm and taut. His shoulders were broad, and his muscles beneath his short sleeves bulged and flexed as he moved the paintbrush back and forth. As she watched, a huge spider danced across the area where he was working. He brushed it away with a nonchalance that made Hannah see red.

"You jerk," she yelled, throwing her paintbrush at him, not caring when the brush struck his blue shirt, leaving a vivid, white streak. "I knew you were lying to me, I just knew it!"

Alex didn't have to ask what was wrong. He knew. He'd known his mistake the instant he'd made it. He climbed down the ladder and turned to face her, his guilt written all over his face.

"You lied," she repeated, her expression full of indignation. "You aren't afraid of spiders."

"Hannah, I was going to tell you...."

"When? After the session today? After the one tomorrow? After I wasted six hours of my time on you? What is this, some sort of game with you? Don't you understand? This is my work. The time I wasted with you I could have used to help somebody who really needed it."

"I'm sorry," he said, and he genuinely meant it. For the first time in as long as he could remember, he felt ashamed. She was right. He had taken advantage of her, used a make-believe illness for his own purposes.

She twirled around and started to head toward the house, anger battling with outrage at his ruse.

"Hannah, please wait. Let me explain." Alex grabbed her arm, not wanting to let her go. He had the feeling that if she walked away from him at this moment, he would never get an opportunity to get close to her again.

She turned around and faced him, her eyes muddled with emotion. "I don't play games, Alex. I don't have the time or the patience for them."

"I didn't mean to play games. You're right, I lied. I'm not afraid of spiders. I don't need a therapist." He moved forward and took her hand in his. "But I could use a friend."

"A man like you must have lots of friends," she scoffed, but the anger in her eyes was fading and she had stopped fighting to get away from him.

"No, I don't. I have a lot of acquaintances who want something from me, people who appease me because I'm the boss, but I don't have any real friends." He hadn't realized it was true until he said the words, and the bleakness he felt as he spoke was reflected in his voice.

Hannah recognized the bleakness and her anger dissipated. Instead, she realized that in him was the same loneliness she had felt. "Do you even know how to be a friend?" she asked guardedly.

"I'm not sure," he admitted thoughtfully. "Couldn't you teach me?"

Hannah looked at him for a long moment. Could she be friends with this man who stood for so many things she didn't believe in? Could they find some common ground that could result in a friendship, and not step over that line? "Okay," she finally agreed. Perhaps this is best, she told herself. Being friends. After all, friends don't break each other's hearts.

Chapter Four

"Miranda, darling. I came tonight because I promised you I'd escort you to the opening," Alex explained patiently as he maneuvered his sports car around a corner, heading for the off-Broadway theater. "But I'm not driving back into the city tomorrow night," he finished by saying.

Miranda's nostrils flared, the only indication of her displeasure at his words. "Mother and Father will be very disappointed. They were looking forward to our having dinner with them."

"We'll just have to make it another night. I don't intend on spending my entire vacation driving back and forth from the island to the city." He looked over at her. She was staring straight ahead, her nostrils flared even more widely. She'd been irritated with him ever since he'd picked her up in the little sports car. She'd wanted the limo with Jacob serving as chauffeur to take them to the theater so they would arrive in the manner that befitted her position as "angel." Backing obscure plays and unknown playwrights was Miranda's pet hobby. "Are your parents attending tonight?" he asked.

"Of course. So are the Wainwrights, the Delafields and the Burrmans. I also sent an invitation to Max Wilding."

Alex smiled at her. "Great. If he comes maybe I can pin him down on a few points at the party after the play."

Alex fell silent, his thoughts going over all he knew of Max Wilding. Alex had been working with lawyers for the past month to acquire Wilding Electronics, but he had yet to meet the elusive owner, Max, in person. According to Alex's information, Max was a poor farmboy who'd started the business in his Kansas barn. Within ten years he'd made enough money to move East and compete with nationally known electronics companies. Now word was out that Max, at sixty-eight years old, was looking to sell. But he wasn't at all sure he wanted to sell to Alex, and therein lay the reason that it had become a company Alex meant to have.

"I suppose this also means you won't be driving in this Friday night for the Impressionist painting exhibition." Miranda interrupted his thoughts.

"No, I won't. I told you not to make any plans for me while I was on vacation." He glanced over to her again. Had she always gotten that pinched look when she was perturbed? Must she always maintain such cool control over her emotions? Didn't she ever let her anger sweep over her, causing her eyes to shoot green sparks of anger? He stopped the thought. Of course not, Miranda's eyes were blue.

He looked over at her again, noting the way the diamond necklace around her neck seemed to reflect her personality, sparkling with brilliance but offering no warmth. Miranda would make the perfect corporate wife. She was at ease in social situations, knew the corporate games that had to be played. She would never demand more than he could give. She'd never expect emotional bonding or excess time with her husband. She'd be content to indulge herself in shopping and charity functions and pet projects.

Yes, Miranda would make a perfect wife. So, why was he counting the minutes, the hours until tomorrow morning when he would see Hannah again? After she'd agreed to be his friend, he'd talked her into inviting him over for coffee the next morning, the first step toward forming a relationship. Of course, the last thing he wanted from Hannah was a real friendship. What he had in mind was a relationship a little less lasting and much more exciting.

Hannah certainly wasn't a diamond. She was much more like an opal, offering subtle glimpses of passion and emotion, depths and colors sparking from within. Hannah would be the worse kind of corporate wife. She would never understand the importance of work, never understand the forces that drove a man like

himself. So, why, knowing that Hannah was all wrong
for him, was he anticipating the morning so intensely?

Hannah sat at the table, making notes on the pre-
vious day's session with Carrie. She frowned as she
realized there wasn't much to note. Although with
each session, Carrie seemed more relaxed, more enamored with Peter Rabbit, she had yet to utter a single word. After yesterday's session, Carrie's father had
called, wondering why no progress was being made.
Hannah had explained to him that therapy took time,
that results couldn't be expected after only three sessions. He had explained to her that he had an ex-
tended business trip planned to the Orient in two
weeks and he would like Carrie's problems solved by
then.

She now set down her pencil and rubbed her forehead. What did the man expect her to do? Wave a
magic wand? Did he want immediate results, like instant pudding? Take a troubled child, add a pinch of
psychologist, stir and poof, instant success. Well,
Carrie's father was going to discover things didn't
work that quickly or that easily.

She closed her notebook and thought of the other
man who was causing her troubling thoughts. Alex.
She'd been so angry with him the day before when
she'd realized he'd lied about his arachnophobia. Initially, she'd been suspicious, but when he'd finally
confessed, she'd felt betrayed, like she was the pawn
in a game she didn't understand. But then, when he'd

asked her to be his friend, a part of her heart that had remained chilled for so long had warmed and expanded. However, with a good night's sleep behind her, she was beginning to wonder if she hadn't made a mistake in agreeing to be his friend.

Although Hannah didn't believe in astrological charting and horoscopes as completely as Edna, she did believe that certain personality traits ran true to certain signs. Impatient, insensitive, restless... she'd had too many years of living with Edward and his Arian peculiarities to want to get involved with another of the ram sign.

It was like a bunny rabbit trying to be friends with a scorpion. Sooner or later the scorpion was going to sting, because that was the nature of the beast. And sooner or later, Alex would hurt her, because that was his nature... wasn't it?

She opened the paper to the society pages, looking at the picture of Alex and Miranda Weatherford attending a play performance. This was the second time this week they had been photographed together. Was Alex serious about this cool, arrogant-looking blonde? It would seem so.

Hannah briskly shut the paper and folded it back to its original form. She didn't care who Alex saw socially. She didn't care whom he married, whom he lived with for the rest of his life. He professed that he wanted to be her friend, but she had a feeling he was merely interested in the novelty of such a relationship. When his vacation ended, it would be back to business as usual for him, and Hannah would be shunted aside for more important things.

Still, there was a part of her that wished she could impart to him some of the same sort of inner peace she'd found. She wished she could give him a new set of values, ones that would make his life rich and full, yet had nothing to do with money or business successes.

"Hi."

She jumped at the sound of his voice at the kitchen door. "Hi. I didn't hear you come in," she said, slightly flustered by his sudden appearance when her thoughts had been so full of him only seconds before.

"Edna let me in with her usual friendly flare." He joined her at the table, and once again Hannah was struck by what an attractive man he was. More than that, there was something in his gaze that made her aware of herself as a woman. He brought out a femininity she hadn't realized was inside her. She wasn't sure she was comfortable with the way he made her feel.

"Let me get you a cup of coffee," Hannah said, starting to get up.

"I'll get his coffee," Edna replied, bustling into the kitchen and grabbing the coffeepot. She poured his coffee and set it down before him. "I met your man at the store early this morning."

"My man?" Alex looked at her blankly, then smiled. "Oh, you mean Jacob." He picked up his cup.

Edna nodded. "He's an uptight old poop, isn't he?"

Alex nearly choked on his coffee, imagining Jacob's horror at such a description of himself.

"Where is he from, anyway?" Edna asked curiously.

Alex stared at her for a long moment, surprised by her question, but even more surprised to realize he wasn't sure of the answer. "He's worked for my family for as long as I can remember."

"Does he have any family?"

"I don't know. I'm not sure."

"And you've never bothered to find out?" Hannah looked at him in astonishment.

"Sure, I've tried, but Jacob gets real uncomfortable when I ask him questions about his personal life. He doesn't think it's seemly for me to bother myself with the details of his life."

Hannah sighed. "This merely emphasizes the differences in our priorities, in our life-styles." She was vaguely aware of Edna leaving the kitchen. Leave it to Edna to stir up a whirlwind, then retreat to a safe distance. Still, Hannah was grateful to the old woman for bringing up this particular point, bringing home to Hannah once again how very different she and Alex were, how ridiculous it was for them to try to find common ground and forge a friendship. "Alex," she began hesitantly. "You and I come from totally different worlds. There has to be some sort of a common basis to form a friendship."

"We're neighbors. Isn't that a basis?" he asked.

She shook her head with a sad smile. "You told me yesterday that you don't have any friends. I believe that you can't be a friend to another person until you learn to be a friend to yourself, and I don't think you've discovered yourself as a friend yet.''

''I'm not sure I understand what you mean.'' Alex pushed his cup of coffee aside and gave her his full attention. He wasn't sure what was happening, but it smelled like defeat, a scent that he knew from experience would burn for a long time in his nose.

''When was the last time you spent time by yourself?''

''I spend lots of time by myself,'' he protested.

''I mean time where you talk to yourself about your hopes and dreams, about ultimate goals and decisions, ones that have nothing to do with your business.'' She smiled as he looked at her blankly. ''Yes, you heard me. Nothing to do with business.'' She leaned forward, looking at him intently. ''If you really want to be my friend, then you need to become your own best friend first, and to do that, I have an exercise I'd like you to do.''

''An exercise?'' He looked at her skeptically. ''They have exercises for making friendships?''

She laughed, deciding it was really a stroke of genius. She'd give him an opportunity to do things her way, and if she read his character right, he would tire of both her and her games and go back to his high-stress, immediate gratification world where he thought he was happy. She stood up and went to the kitchen window, motioning for him to join her there.

''See that ridge, the one between my property and yours?''

He leaned toward her, looking to where she was pointing. God, she smelled good, like an exotic flower from the Pacific Islands. He was standing close enough to her to feel the heat that emanated from her body, a heat that beckoned him closer.

"Do you see it?" she asked, pulling him from his pleasant game of trying to imagine the way her body would look on the silken sheets of his bed.

"Yeah, I see it," he answered.

"I'd like for you to take an hour and sit up there." She flushed under his gaze. When he looked at her like that she felt as though she were a delicious cheesecake and he had an insatiable sweet tooth that only cheesecake could satisfy.

"Sit up there and do what?" he asked, wondering if she was teasing him, but one look at her assured him she was perfectly serious.

"I want you to sit up there and look around, and let your mind run free. Think about where you're going and where you've been in your personal life."

"Then what?" Personally, he thought the whole thing sounded like a ridiculous waste of time.

"Then you and I can talk about it," she answered.

"If I go up there and sit this afternoon, then can we talk about it tonight over dinner at my house?" He'd be willing to give up an hour of his time this afternoon if it meant he could be alone with her this evening. He smiled, already thinking of a candlelit dinner, champagne flowing freely, a lowering of inhibitions, a rising of passions. Ah, the taste of success—he could already savor the flavor on his lips.

"Okay," she agreed reluctantly. What harm was there in one dinner? "But only if you do as I ask."

He nodded and grinned at her. "I guess I'd better take off."

"But you haven't finished your coffee," Hannah said, surprised at his brief visit.

"I don't have time for coffee. I've got a hill to sit on." With a jaunty wave, he headed for the front door.

Hannah walked into the living room, stopped at the window just in time to see his sports car shooting up the driveway. She'd been crazy to agree to have dinner with him. Of course, if her plan worked, he'd spend about ten minutes sitting on the ridge, feel completely ridiculous, then would call her up and cancel the dinner date, thinking that pursuing a relationship with her was too much trouble. She didn't consider what would happen if her plan didn't work. It was too disturbing to consider.

Alex frowned, swatting irritably at a fly who was dive-bombing his head. He squirmed as a bead of sweat slowly trekked down his back, finally absorbing into the waistband of his shorts. He'd been sitting on this ridge for almost thirty minutes, and so far nothing had happened. Well, actually, that wasn't quite true. His behind ached, his ankles were being eaten alive by cannibal ants and his eyes hurt from the constant glare of the bright sunshine. There was definitely no sign yet of pleasant thoughts skittering across his mind.

He crinkled his forehead, trying to make his mind a blank so all these epiphanies of life could enter. That's what Hannah wanted... she wanted the light bulb to go off in his head, make him realize... what?

"Sir? I have your lunch ready."

He turned to see Jacob standing behind him, the old man's expression inscrutable as usual.

"Jacob, why don't you join me?" He motioned for Jacob to sit beside him in the grass. "Hannah says it's good for the soul, to sit out in the fresh air and think."

"Yes, sir." Jacob carefully unbuttoned his dark suit jacket and gingerly sat down beside Alex.

For several minutes the two men sat side by side in silence. "Are you feeling anything?" Alex finally broke the silence, looking at Jacob curiously.

"Only rather ridiculous," Jacob answered.

"My sentiments exactly," Alex said, puffing a deep breath of frustration. "Let's go back to the house." He stood up, brushing off the back of his legs, which had begun to itch with irritating persistence.

"Oh, sir." For the first time in years, Jacob's face held an expression of horror.

"What's the matter?" Alex asked, bending down to scratch the back of his legs once again.

"See that patch where you were sitting?" Jacob pointed. "Note how all three of the leaves look exactly alike?" Alex nodded and Jacob continued. "I believe, sir, what we have there is a big patch of poison ivy."

Chapter Five

Hannah and Edna had just sat down in the living room for their customary afternoon cup of coffee when there was a knock at the door. "I'll get it," Hannah said, jumping up before the older woman could protest.

She answered, unsurprised to see Jacob, the man who worked for Alex, standing on the porch. She'd been expecting him, anticipating Alex's decision to forget their deal. Jacob's first words proved her correct.

"Mr. Donaldson requested that I come over to extend his apologies. He will have to postpone your dinner date for this evening."

"Oh, I was so looking forward to it," Hannah replied with a small smile. She'd been right in her assessment of Alexander Donaldson as a man who wouldn't want to work too hard for a personal relationship. If there was no monetary gain, no effort was worth it.

"I'm afraid Mr. Donaldson is rather ill disposed, but he should be feeling better in a couple of days."

"Mr. Donaldson is ill? I hope it isn't anything serious," Hannah replied, wondering if it was merely an excuse or if Alex was really sick.

"The doctor assured him he should feel better in a couple of days."

"The doctor?" Edna joined them at the door. "What's wrong with him that he needed a doctor?"

Jacob hesitated, looking decidedly uncomfortable at the prospect of discussing his employer's illness with the two women.

"For God's sake, spit it out, man," Edna exclaimed, causing a vivid blush to sweep over the man's face.

"Mr. Donaldson was sitting on the hillside enjoying being outside in the fresh air. Unfortunately, beneath him was a rather large patch of poison ivy."

Hannah could have sworn she saw a ghost of a humorous twinkle in Jacob's eyes, but she had no time to consider it as a wave of guilt swept over her. It was all her fault.

She was the one who had instructed Alex to sit on the ridge.

"Poison ivy?" Edna echoed, then snorted impatiently. "Damn fool man. Doesn't he know the difference between poison ivy and grass?"

"It would appear he doesn't," Jacob replied stiffly.

Edna studied Jacob for a moment, then sniffed again with the same impatience. "What's the doctor doing for him?"

"He prescribed some tablets for him to take."

"Pills, bah. Pills don't do any good once you've contracted the stuff. Wait here," Edna instructed, then she quickly disappeared into the kitchen.

"Would you like to come in?" Hannah asked him, unsurprised when he declined. He stood, as if at attention, with his hat in his hand, looking shy and uncomfortable. Hannah tried to think of something to say to put him at ease. "Was Mr. Donaldson angry?"

"Only with himself," Jacob returned. "He feels very foolish, and that's a feeling Mr. Donaldson doesn't like."

"I can imagine," Hannah said dryly.

At that moment, Edna returned, carrying several containers of mysterious ingredients. "This is the best thing I know for poison ivy. This won't cure it, but it will help ease the itching and irritability." She handed Jacob three containers. "Now, this one you put in a hot bath. Just sprinkle it in the water and make him soak in it for about fifteen minutes. This smaller one is for tea. A teaspoon in a cup of water should do the trick. And this one..." Edna suddenly waved her hands impatiently. "This will never do. You'll just have to take us over there and let me treat Mr. Donaldson myself."

Jacob was taken aback. "Oh, I don't know if that's prudent...I'm not sure Mr. Donaldson would want..."

"Mr. Donaldson would want to feel better, now wouldn't he? Hannah, get my pocketbook." Edna left no room for any more arguments, but instead grabbed the containers from Jacob, then walked to the car and planted herself in the front seat.

"There's no sense arguing with her when she gets this way," Hannah said to the astonished Jacob. "She has her mind set."

"She seems to be a woman of strong will," Jacob observed.

Hannah laughed at his diplomatic assessment. Her smile slowly faded and she frowned thoughtfully. "Perhaps I'd better come along. We might need a buffer between Edna and Alex, and besides, I owe Alex an apology." And she escorted Jacob out of the house.

It took only minutes for the three of them to arrive back at Alex's. "Jacob, is that you?" Alex's voice bellowed from somewhere above them as they walked into the entry hall.

"Yes, Mr. Donaldson," he returned, then looked at the two women. "Perhaps it would be best if I'd prepare him for your visit." He started for the staircase, but paused as Edna hurried to get in front of him.

"He doesn't need preparing. All he needs is what I've got right here. I'll take care of him." With these words, she thundered up the stairs, her shoulders set with grim determination.

"What the he—" Alex's words were cut short as a door was slammed shut.

Jacob and Hannah stared at each other, Jacob's face holding a look of such horror that Hannah found herself sympathetic with the man.

"Surely Alex won't be angry with you." She tried to console him.

"Oh, I'm not worried about that. I just hope Ms. Edna doesn't hurt Mr. Donaldson." Jacob blushed, as if unaccustomed to expressing his thoughts aloud.

Hannah laughed. "I wouldn't worry about that. She'll be firm, but gentle."

"Perhaps you'd like to wait in here." Jacob led her into the room where she had sat the first time she had been here to discuss her errant sheep. "Could I bring you something to eat or drink?"

"No thank you, Jacob. I'll be fine," Hannah said, assuring him.

With a stiff nod, Jacob withdrew, closing the door and leaving her alone. There was an ominous silence from the rooms above, and Hannah found herself pacing restlessly. She had to admit, she was surprised and somehow vaguely pleased that Alex had actually tried what she had recommended. He'd actually meant to carry through on their bargain. He'd gone to sit on that ridge and in turn she would have had to uphold her end of the deal by sharing dinner with him.

Perhaps it was best that Alex had contracted poison ivy and their date for this evening had been cancelled. She'd never expected him to follow through on this anyway. She didn't want to have dinner with him.

She didn't want to have anything to do with him. They were from two different worlds, had two completely different value systems and there was no point in trying to mesh them. Maybe Alex's poison ivy was a sign that any kind of relationship between them would be as ill-fated as his attempts to sit on the ridge and contemplate his life-style.

She studied her surroundings. No place were their different worlds more evident than from where she stood. This room, this very house, epitomized everything she had left behind her when she'd divorced Edward. The fine furnishings, the expensive paintings on the walls, the original sculptures beneath glass cases, were evidence of a life-style far removed from her own. This was a house for show, not for warmth and living.

She walked over to the bookshelves, unsurprised to see that most of the books were expensive first editions and antiques. Her gaze was caught by a floral-bound volume that looked conspicuously out of place among the others. She pulled it out, and was surprised to see that it was a photo album.

Opening it, she studied the first photograph, finding herself looking at a picture of a couple. It was easy to guess that the man was Alex's father—the physical resemblance was uncanny. The woman was ethereal looking, with a halo of blond hair and a childlike innocence in her brilliant blue eyes. Alex's mother?

Hannah flipped to the next page, discovering the answer to her question. The next photo was of the same woman holding a little boy. He had Alex's firm chin, his dark hair and his eyes.

She turned to the next page and a small smile unconsciously curved her lips. It was another picture of Alex and his mother, a memory caught on celluloid, capturing the relationship between mother and child. They were sitting on a beach, Alex covering his mother's legs with sand. Hannah guessed that Alex was about eight years old, and there was an expression on his face of such adoration, such a love of living, that her heart ached as she wondered what had happened to turn that little boy into a somber, driven businessman. And more importantly, was it possible that this little boy was someplace deep inside Alex, just waiting for an opportunity to break free and enjoy living once again?

Feeling like she was snooping, Hannah closed the photo album and placed it back among the books where it had been.

She whirled around as the door opened and Alex entered the room. He was clad in a loose-fitting pair of pajamas and a robe, the belt dangling untied at the sides. He strode purposely across the room directly over to a portable bar in one corner of the room. He poured two fingers of an amber liquid into a goblet, downed it, then slammed the glass down on the bar and turned to glare at her. "This is all your fault," he accused.

"You're absolutely right," Hannah agreed evenly. She could tell by the muscle working erratically at his jawline that he was in no mood to argue.

"And that woman—" He jerked a thumb in the direction of the other room. "She could find employment as a sergeant in the Marine Corps."

"Where is Edna now?" Hannah asked.

"Who knows, probably rearranging the kitchen cabinets. She's already redone my bathroom linen closet." Alex frowned irritably. When Edna had burst into his study, he'd been feeling more miserable than he could ever remember in his life. He was rarely ill, usually because he refused to take the time to allow himself an illness. But this poison ivy was something else. It itched and burned and made him feel like he'd lost control. And that, more than anything, was causing his irritability.

He turned back to glare at Hannah, who was the most convenient recipient of his foul mood. "You and your crazy ideas. 'Go sit on the hill,' she says, 'get to know yourself.' I reiterate, this is all your fault."

"And I repeat, I agree," Hannah returned. "I told you to go sit on that hill, hoping you would choose to sit in a patch of poison ivy because basically I'm a mean and vicious person."

Alex stared at her for a moment, then slowly he felt his foul mood evaporating and a smile tugging at his lips. "I'm being childish, aren't I?" He sat down next to her, grimacing slightly as the back of his legs bumped against the edge of the sofa.

"It's been my experience that most men resort to childhood when they don't feel well," she said with a small smile.

"I find that remark objectionably sexist," he replied.

"Perhaps, but it's true. How are you feeling?"

Alex paused thoughtfully before answering. "Actually, I hate to admit it, but Edna's treatment seems to be working. I'm not itching as much as I was." He could smell Hannah's perfume from where he sat. It was a mysterious, woodsy scent that made him remember all his plans for their dinner together. Candlelight, champagne...her mouth beneath his, her body pressed invitingly against him. She looked particularly alluring, dressed simply in a forest-green blouse and slacks that intensified the depth of green in her eyes. "You owe me a dinner," he said, his gaze lingering on the fullness of her lips, disappointed that his plans for the evening had gone awry. "We had a deal, and I upheld my part of the bargain. I sat on that hill, and I tried to contemplate my life and my values, and I can't say I found it a particularly pleasant experience."

"What makes you think having dinner with me would be a pleasant experience?" Hannah asked, wishing he wouldn't stare at her so intently. She stood up suddenly, needing to move around, get away from his gaze, which was making the room seem unusually warm. "So, you didn't learn anything from your experience of sitting alone out in the sunshine?"

"Sure, I learned that I hate sitting alone out in the sunshine." He grinned at her. "Hannah, face it. The experiment was a dismal failure. I'm no good at spending time outside doing nothing but thinking. The only thing I learned about myself that I didn't know before is that I'm allergic to poison ivy."

She laughed. Despite her reservations about developing a relationship with Alex, she couldn't resist his sense of humor and boyish attractiveness. Was he a hopeless case? A man who could never learn the value of things other than money? She suddenly thought of the picture she had seen. The childhood image of him laughing, the exuberant expression on his face, made her believe he had simply lost touch with that inner child. A child whose treasures might have been the sight of a butterfly on a flower, a falling star in the sky.

"Alex, if you wanted to try it again—sitting on the ridge, I mean ... well, I'd be glad to sit with you."

"Tomorrow?"

She nodded.

"Okay," he agreed. "But you still owe me a dinner, say this Friday night. By then most of my itching should be finished."

She laughed again. The man was nothing if not persistent. "Okay, dinner this Friday." She felt a moment of panic the second the words left her mouth. Was she setting herself up again for more heartache? After all, Alex was so much like the Aries men who had caused her such unhappiness in the past. Was she merely falling into an old rut, a bad habit, tempting fate to kick her in the rear end once again?

In any case, there was no opportunity for her to call back her words, as Edna chose that moment to bustle in the room, a cup of steaming brew in her hand.

"Drink this," she commanded, holding the cup out to Alex.

"Why does this scene suddenly bring to mind the memory of a particular fairy tale involving a brightly polished apple?" he asked, accepting the cup from Edna, his words causing Hannah to stifle a giggle. "What is this?" he asked, peering into the cup with a look of distaste.

"Never you mind what it is, you just make sure you drink every drop. And I left some more of that oatmeal bath with Jacob." She looked at Hannah expectantly. "I'd say our business is finished here."

"Yes, we should be getting back home," Hannah agreed.

"I'll have Jacob drive you home," Alex offered, rising up off the sofa.

"Oh, that won't be necessary. We can walk," Hannah demurred.

"Speak for yourself. I'd prefer to be driven," Edna replied. "I'm feeling a touch of arthritis in my hip. It makes walking rather difficult."

Hannah looked at her in surprise. She'd never heard Edna complain about arthritis before. As Alex called for Jacob, Hannah continued to stare at Edna, wondering if it was just her imagination or if there was really a blush of faint color on the older woman's chubby cheeks.

"I think I'll go ahead and walk home," Hannah said as they waited for Jacob.

"Don't forget about tomorrow," Alex reminded her. "We have a date to hill-sit."

Hannah flushed, not sure if she liked him referring to it as a date. "I won't forget. I never mind helping a friend get in touch with himself," she said, hoping her words would let him know where she stood.

Alex grinned. He wasn't interested in getting in touch with himself, but he definitely had a strong urge to get in touch with her. Still, he sensed her erecting an emotional wall, pulling away from him, and he knew better than to push her too far, go too fast. "If nothing else, perhaps you can teach me the difference between weeds and poison ivy."

Hannah relaxed and grinned. "Weren't you ever a Boy Scout?"

"Never had the time," Alex replied, and Hannah wondered if she heard a touch of wistfulness in his voice or if she only imagined it.

"Well, I'll see you tomorrow. Why don't we say around ten."

He nodded and walked with her to the door, where Edna and Jacob were waiting. "You two go ahead, I'm going to walk," Hannah said to them, then turned to Alex. "Well, good night, and I hope you're feeling better tomorrow." With a parting smile, she stepped outside into the evening air. As she started off, she saw Edna getting into the car with Jacob, and Hannah could have sworn she heard the older woman emit a coquettish laugh.

As Hannah made her way across Alex's meticulously manicured lawn, she looked up, searching for the moon. She wouldn't be surprised if it was a full

one. Surely that was the only explanation for the fact
that she'd agreed to sit on a hill with Alex the next day,
and that Edna was giggling like a love-struck teen-
ager.

Chapter Six

"How does this look?" Alex asked, pointing to a grassy area on the side of the ridge.

"Looks much better than wherever it was you sat yesterday," Hannah replied with a smile. "I don't see any suspicious-looking plants around."

"Please, don't remind me." Alex carefully unfolded a blanket and laid it down on the grass, then sat down, motioning for Hannah to join him.

Hannah sat on the edge of the blanket, as far away from him as she could get without ending up on the grass. This was all a mistake. She didn't want to be out here with him. He looked so vital, too handsome with the sunlight dancing in his hair, highlighting the bronzed skin of his forearms. Each time she'd seen him before, there had been a formality about him.

Even in his pajamas the night before, there had been a sort of dignity, an imposing air that came from a man who was accustomed to being in charge. But today, that air was gone, leaving a more vulnerable Alex, one Hannah found threatening in his attractiveness.

"So, what do we do now?" he asked, looking at her curiously.

"Nothing," she answered.

"Nothing?" He looked at her dubiously.

She laughed despite her apprehension. "Yes, Alex. Nothing. I know it's a concept alien to your nature, but try it."

He nodded again, trying to concentrate on nothing, but it was impossible. For one thing, Hannah looked too damned enticing, much too alive for him to ignore. Never had he seen a woman whom the sun seemed to love so much. Most of the women he'd known shunned the brilliance of sunshine, knowing the natural light magnified wrinkles and imperfections. But Hannah wore the sunlight on her face like other women wore diamonds around their necks. She raised her face to it, like one seeking the touch of a lover. Rather than finding imperfections, Alex marveled in the smoothness of her skin, the clearness of her eyes. She was unlike any woman he'd ever been with before, and once again he found himself trying to discern the key that would unleash the passion he sensed shimmered just beneath her surface.

He fought an impulse to reach out and touch the shining cap of her hair, smell the heady fragrance of her. He had sensed her apprehension from the moment he'd arrived at her front door and he knew that if he moved too fast, he would frighten her off.

"It's a beautiful day, isn't it?" Hannah said softly, breaking the spell of silence that had fallen between them.

"I guess," he replied, for the first time noting how the sunshine made their surroundings seem more vivid, the colors of nature much sharper. "Actually, I rarely spend much time outdoors," he admitted. "An occasional tennis game or a day of sailing..." He smiled ruefully. "And usually the thing uppermost in my mind is how quickly I can get back to work."

"You love your work that much?" Hannah raised her knees up to her chest and wrapped her arms around them.

"Sure," he answered without hesitation. He stretched out on his back, staring up at the sky. "My work is my life." He'd always taken great pride in his work, but as he said these words, he realized how hollow they sounded, how empty. "I love my work," he said with more emphasis, as if to banish any momentary unease he felt. "I find it stimulating, challenging."

"Tell me about it," she prompted. She wasn't sure whether she genuinely wanted to know, or if it was merely that she enjoyed the sound of his voice, a resonant bass that created the same tingling sensations as a big drum passing by her in a parade.

"Right now I'm trying to negotiate the buy-out of an electronics company, Wilding Electronics. Max Wilding, the man who owns it, is a headstrong, stubborn fool." Alex sat up, his features more animated than they'd been all morning. "Max had big ideas, and overexpanded the company. Now it's facing a cash-flow problem and he's decided the only way out is to sell. I want the company."

"Why?" The one-word question caused Alex to look at her in surprise. "I mean, if the company is having cash-flow problems and has overextended itself, why would you want it?" she continued. "Wouldn't you have to put a lot of money and work into the company to make it solvent?"

"Sure, but it could eventually be a solid investment."

"And you need more investments?"

"Well, not really." Alex ran a hand through his hair, trying to find the words to use to explain to Hannah why he wanted the company. The funny thing was, he couldn't even find the words to explain it to himself. He finally settled by saying, "I just want that company, that's all." Flushing, he realized it made him sound like a spoiled child. "You love your work, don't you?" he asked her, as if to defend himself.

"Sure, but my work is not my life," Hannah stated.

"Don't you believe in ambition?" Alex moved closer to her, as if he could make her understand his position in the world of business by sheer persistence and fervor.

"Of course," she answered immediately. "But, I also believe in balance. You seem to be a man who has lost his balance. You've totally immersed yourself in work and lost touch with everything else that matters in life."

"That's why I'm here with you right now." He moved even closer to her, reaching out to trace one finger down the length of her arm. "You're going to put the balance back in my life, remind me that there are other things besides work." He saw the way her eyes darkened, going from their sea-green color to a deep jade. God, how he wanted her. How he would love to lay her down on this blanket and make love to her with the sun and the sky as witnesses. He'd love to feel her moving beneath him, to watch as her eyes spoke the language of passion.

"Lie down on your back," she said suddenly, moving out of his reach.

"What?"

"Lie down on your back, like you were a minute ago," she explained, watching as he did as she asked. Then she did the same, stretching out beside him, keeping enough distance between them that their bodies didn't touch. "Have you ever sat and watched the clouds, tried to discern shapes of things?"

"I can't say that I have," Alex replied dryly, thinking the whole idea sounded rather ridiculous.

"Try it now. See if you can find the shapes of things in the clouds." Hannah lay on her back, staring up at the sky, but her thoughts were not on the puffy, white cottonlike balls that hung as if suspended on a blue backdrop. Rather, her mind was full of Alex, and the way his light touch on her arm had made her insides quiver in anticipation. She was intensely aware of him next to her. His body emitted a heat that had nothing to do with the sun overhead.

Everything she learned about him, everything he said, only served to remind her of how much she didn't want to become involved with a man like Alex. The disillusionment of her marriage still tasted sour in her mouth, and yet she couldn't deny that something was at work between them, some attraction that refused to be denied.

She studiously pulled her mind from these kinds of thoughts and stared at the clouds overhead. "I see an elephant riding a bicycle," she said, finding the image in a distant puff of white._"Do you see anything?"

Alex leaned up on one elbow and studied her, a tiny smile curving his lips upward. "Is this sort of like the ink-blot tests? Are you going to analyze everything I say I see in the clouds?"

"What do you mean?" Hannah asked curiously, noting how the sun picked up the auburn glints in his thick hair.

"If I see a woman rocking a cradle, will you discern some sort of Freudian connotation, like I wasn't breast-fed long enough as a baby?"

Hannah laughed. "No, there's nothing psychological about cloud watching, it's just a pleasant way to spend time."

"Good, because I think that cloud over there looks exactly like a dollar sign, and the one there by the trees looks like a stack of gold coins." Hannah looked at him suspiciously to see if he was teasing her. Sure enough, there was a mischievous twinkle in his eyes. "Well, those are the kinds of things you expect me to see, isn't it?"

"Of course not, I expect you to see whatever you see," she protested, although he was half-right. "I just wanted you to realize that there are other things in life besides work. That it's okay to spend time looking at clouds, or enjoying the sight of a sunset."

"In other words, you want me to learn to stop and smell the roses," Alex replied. Hannah nodded. "But what you don't understand is that I'd much rather smell you," he said softly, and before Hannah realized his intentions, he leaned over her and softly claimed her lips with his. For a long moment, nothing touched but their mouths. Then with a small groan of pleasure, Alex moved so that his chest was on top of hers, and his arms gathered her closer as he deepened the kiss.

Hannah knew she should stop this, that they were moving beyond the barriers she had tried to erect, but desire battled with good sense, and in the end desire won. She returned his kiss, loving the way the tip of his tongue outlined her upper lip, then teased its way into her mouth. She reveled in the feel of his chest leaning heavily against her own, his heartbeat whispering to hers as his hand moved between them to cup one of her breasts through the sweatshirt she was wearing.

"Oh, Hannah," he moaned softly in her ear. "I want you."

The words, spoken in the same tone of voice as he'd used when he'd spoke of the Wilding Electronics

Company, caused a semblance of sanity to return to her.

"Alex ... I ..." She pushed him away from her and sat up. "I have to get back ... I have a patient coming in just a few minutes...." She looked at her watch and stood up, confused by the myriad of emotions racing through her.

Too fast, Alex thought as he saw the bewilderment on her face. He'd moved much too fast, letting his emotions get in the way of his good sense. "Okay," he replied, allowing her the escape she sought. "You go ahead. I'll pick up the blanket."

She nodded, grateful for his tact in not wanting to discuss what had just transpired between them. She turned to leave, but paused as he called her name.

"I have to drive into the city for some business tomorrow, but I'm still planning on our dinner date Friday night. Shall we say around six?"

She hesitated, good sense dictating that she say no, but she had made a promise. "Okay, Friday at six," she agreed.

"I'll have Jacob pick you up."

"Thanks, but I prefer to walk." Then Hannah turned and headed for home. She would fulfill her promise to dine with him, and she would make sure the dinner was the end of their relationship. She refused to have her heart broken by a man who saw dollar signs in the clouds.

Alex watched her walking away, his gaze thoughtful. She disturbed him, more than he'd ever been in his life. On the surface, their conversation had been simple, one-dimensional, but she'd made him think about things he'd never thought about before, like the Wilding buy-out. She'd also made him feel things he'd never felt before. He believed that if he'd pressed it, he could have made love to her right here on this hillside. But he hadn't wanted her that way, with her mind confused. When he made love to her, he wanted her coming to him with her mind clear, her desire uncomplicated by any other emotions.

Alex smiled, remembering the velvety softness of her lips against his, the way she had responded to him. This was one merger Alex was definitely looking forward to, more than any in his life.

Friday evening arrived all too quickly to please Hannah. As she dressed for her dinner date with Alex, she went over in her mind all the reasons she didn't want to get involved with him. But, no matter what reasons she came up with, they seemed to lose their importance as she remembered his kiss.

It had been a very long time since Hannah had felt the stirrings of desire. Sex had never been high on Edward's priority list, even during the best of times in their marriage. However, Alex's touch, his kiss, had made her remember the romantic, wildly passionate fantasies she'd once believed in, before her marriage had brought her to face harsh reality.

Still, despite her reservation, she dressed with care, choosing a celery-green sundress that she knew brought out the green in her eyes and emphasized her slender waist.

"Humph, terribly dressy for a simple dinner with a neighbor," Edna commented as Hannah stepped into the living room.

"This isn't dressy," Hannah protested, nervously fingering the skirt of her dress.

"Trouble...mark my words, I smell trouble," Edna retorted.

"Maybe it isn't trouble you're smelling, maybe it's your arthritis rub," Hannah returned with a knowing smirk. "You know, the same arthritis that's made it so difficult for you to drive yourself to the grocery store the last couple of days, forcing you to ride with Jacob."

"Well, I have been feeling a touch down in the hip." Edna sniffed defensively, a faint touch of color to her cheeks. "All I'm saying is that you better watch your step. I don't want to see you getting hurt again."

Hannah stepped over to the older woman and kissed her soundly on the forehead. "I know, don't you worry about me. I'm fully in control of this situation." She looked at her wristwatch. "I'd better go."

"Isn't Jacob coming after you?"

Hannah shook her head. "I told Alex I'd walk up. The evenings are so gorgeous, I don't mind."

Edna walked with her to the door. "Be careful. Enjoy your meal...just make sure you aren't dessert," Edna advised, causing Hannah to laugh as she walked out the door.

Hannah did feel fully in control until the moment Alex opened his front door to greet her. As she gazed at him, resplendent in a gray-striped Oxford shirt and gray slacks, she felt her control slip a notch.

"Come in," he said, his gaze sweeping over her, his eyes showing his approval of her appearance. "You look lovely," he observed, leading her into the living room.

He'd done something to the lighting—it was softer, dimmer, and soft music played unobtrusively, creating a pleasing atmosphere. He gestured for her to have a seat, then went over to the bar. "Drink?"

She nodded. "A glass of wine?" She really didn't care what she had to drink, she merely wanted something to do with her hands, something to hold. The subtle lighting, the soft music, all were designed to create an intimate setting, but Hannah refused to be seduced by such artificial means.

She murmured her thanks as he handed her a glass of wine, then joined her on the sofa. "I hope you're feeling better."

He smiled and nodded. "I have to admit, Edna is nothing short of a miracle worker. Whatever it was in those little containers of hers, it did the trick. The poison ivy is almost completely gone."

"That's good." She took a sip of the wine, conscious of his gaze lingering on her. "I hope your trip into the city yesterday went well."

"It went great. I think we've almost got Max Wilding right where we want him." He looked at her expectantly, waiting for words of praise.

Instead she merely shrugged her shoulders. "That's great... if that's what you really want."

At her guarded response, Alex suddenly realized he didn't know anymore exactly what he wanted. Yesterday, while his lawyer had been going over the terms and conditions of the buy-out attempt, he found his thoughts drifting. What was he doing, considering buying another company when he already had so many that he was required to do the work of three men just to stay on top of everything?

This thought had frightened him because it was so alien to what he'd always believed. He'd quickly shoved it aside and had renewed his vigor in discussing the buy-out with his lawyer.

"It's exactly what I want," he now said to Hannah, more sharply than he intended. He tempered the sharpness of his answer with a warm, genuine smile. "Now, tell me what you did the past few days. Have you made any progress with the patient who saw her mother killed in the accident?"

Hannah shook her head, an expression of such sadness on her face that Alex immediately felt his heart constrict in sympathy.

"Every day she's more in touch with her surroundings. There's more eye contact and she's less withdrawn, but she still hasn't uttered a word." Hannah sighed heavily. "I just can't seem to find the key to unlock her silence." She started as his hand covered one of hers warmly.

"It must be so frustrating for you, to be so close to breaking through, yet not quite there." Not only was his hand warm on hers, but his eyes were, as well. Hannah had never known the pleasure of feeling someone else's support, but that was the emotion she felt he was offering her. It was a precious gift, one that lowered her defenses and made her feel more responsive to him.

Her positive feelings toward him continued when Jacob told them dinner was ready and they moved into the dining room.

Again the lights were low, the scene intimate, but Hannah hardly noticed. She was captivated by the fact that Alex seemed more relaxed, more open than she'd ever seen him.

The conversation was light and easy as Alex entertained her with stories of eccentric business associates past and present. Again, Hannah found herself drawn to his sense of humor, which colored his eyes to a warm caramel and banished the aggressive lines she'd first noticed on his face.

By the time they returned to the living room for an after-dinner brandy, Hannah was relaxed and at ease.

"Do you play?" she asked, approaching the piano that stood at one end of the room.

"No, my mother did." Alex handed her the drink and for a moment Hannah wondered if he was going to close up, change the subject. His face darkened, his eyes clouded and he cleared his throat. "She used to play after dinner. She'd always say that the food fed her stomach, but music fed her soul." He looked somewhat astonished. "I'd forgotten all about that," he said softly.

"You were very close to your mother." It was more of a statement than a comment as Hannah remembered the photo she'd seen of Alex and his mother together.

There was a distant look in his eyes. "I sometimes wonder if when I lost my mother, I lost everything good in life." He laughed suddenly and swiped one hand through his hair in a gesture that spoke volumes of his unease. "God, we're getting ridiculously maudlin."

Hannah set down her brandy glass and approached him. She lay a hand against his cheek and gazed into his eyes, eyes that were desperately trying to conceal the emotions inside. "Alex, don't minimize your grief."

He started to protest, but emotion had lodged in his throat, making it impossible for him to speak. It had been a very long time since he had entertained thoughts of his mother, and it was as if Hannah's giving him permission to do so had allowed the grief to surface for the first time since his mother's death so many years earlier.

For a long moment he stood there, letting memories sweep over him, allowing grief to engulf him, and just when he thought he was going to do the unforgivable and lose complete control, Hannah moved into his arms and embraced him.

She was warm against him, the warmth easing the coldness of his grief and effectively banishing all thoughts of his mother.

"Hannah." He groaned her name in her ear and when she looked up at him, he knew she was seeing something very different than what she had seen moments before.

"Hannah." He spoke her name again, watching as her eyes darkened in hue in response to him. The unconscious reaction ignited the smoldering embers of passion that had appeared the moment she had moved into his arms.

His lips met hers, tentatively at first, like the feel of eyelashes fluttering against a cheek. Then, he deepened the kiss, one hand reaching up to tangle in the short, silken strands of her hair while the other hand pressed her more tightly again the length of him.

Hannah was lost, drawn unconditionally into the fire of his eyes, the heat of his kiss. All her reservations, all her uncertainties melted away as she found herself responding to his touch, listening to the hunger that surged through his veins.

His mouth coaxed and pulled a languid yearning from her, creating a need she didn't know existed within her. She leaned into him, reveling in the way his body seemed to surround her, engulf her in warmth as sensuous as silken sheets in front of a roaring fire. She could hear the pounding of his heart, her own answering like primitive drums in a dense jungle.

She sighed in disappointment as he pulled away from her, and she realized the pounding she had heard was Jacob knocking on the living room door.

"Sir, there's a call for you," Jacob said from the doorway.

"Take a message," Alex replied with a touch of impatience.

"Sir, it's a Mr. Max Wilding."

Alex hesitated, then smiled at Hannah in apology. "This should just take a moment." With these words, he followed Jacob out the door, leaving Hannah alone.

She stared at the closed door, numbed firstly by the desire that still tingled throughout her body, and secondly by how quickly, how easily he had walked out.

She reached up and touched her lips, knowing they were swollen and red, testimony to the kisses they'd just shared. Kisses that had meant nothing...ones that had been easily interrupted for a business call. Like a typical Aries, he thought he had her in the palm of his hand and so was now off and running to pursue another goal. He'd left her without thought, inconsiderate of her feelings. As a Cancer woman, to whom emotions ran deep and strong, Hannah knew she was a fool to get involved with another Aries man, who usually left hurt feelings and damaged egos in his wake.

What a fool she'd been, to allow herself to be seduced by his show of emotion, his momentary vulnerability. It was the same old rut, the same old mistake of her past, and she decided at that moment it was a game she didn't want to play.

Chapter Seven

"I'm sorry, Hannah. The call took longer..." Alex entered the room apologizing, but stopped when he realized he was alone. "Hannah?" He turned as Jacob came in.

"Sir, Ms. Martinof went home," the older man announced. "She asked that I give you a message."

"What?"

"She told me to tell you...'priorities.'"

Alex stared at Jacob blankly for a long moment. "That's it?"

Jacob nodded solemnly.

"Thanks, Jacob," Alex replied, running a hand through his hair in frustration. When Jacob left, Alex began to pace. He moved restlessly across the thick carpeting, unable to believe that Hannah had actually walked out on him. Fifteen minutes—he hadn't been on the phone any more than that. What had she expected? That he not take the call? That the world come to a halt while he was spending time with her?

"Good riddance," he mumbled beneath his breath, stalking over to the stereo to shut off the romantic music wafting in the air. He then fully flipped on the lights that he had dimmed to seduction level, flooding the room with harsh reality.

The woman was crazy. Her expectations were too unrealistic. He was first a businessman. He frowned suddenly. Or was he first simply a man?

"Damn," he bellowed. She was making him crazy. He didn't even know who or what he was anymore. She was making him doubt all the things in his life that were most important. He didn't need her around.

He sank down on the sofa, noting her brandy glass on the coffee table in front of him. He picked it up and stared at it. At some point during the night she had sipped from it, because there was a faint smear of pink lipstick on the edge of the glass. The same whisper of pink that had colored her lips. Seeing it made him think of the kiss they had shared just before Jacob had interrupted them. What a kiss it had been, containing all the passion he'd sensed was brimming inside her. Simmering just beneath the surface.

Priorities. A one-word message that spoke volumes of the kind of woman Hannah was. He'd been correct in his first assessment of her. She would make a horrible corporate wife.

So why was he going to go over to her house and try to make amends? Was it because he'd set her up as a goal, and he'd never been satisfied if he didn't achieve his goals? Was she simply a challenge that he refused to deny himself? Or was it that she made him remember that there were things not tangible, things that didn't appear on a spreadsheet, but were equally important to the growth and welfare of a man.

She'd started him on a trip to learn about himself, then had abandoned him along the side of the road. She owed him more of an explanation than just disappearing into the night and leaving behind a one-word message.

"Jacob?" Alex stood up from the sofa, decision made.

Immediately the man stood in the doorway. "Sir?"

"I'm going to Hannah's place."

The older man nodded. "I'll bring the car around."

"No. I'll walk."

"Walk?" Jacob looked surprised.

"Yes, I need the time to think, time to figure out why I'm even wasting my time on Ms. Hannah Martinof."

"Yes, sir," Jacob replied, and for a moment Alex thought he saw a faint smile on the old man's mouth. He didn't take the time to interpret it, but instead walked out the front door, heading for Hannah's.

The night was dark, with the moon hiding beneath the cover of thick clouds, peeking out only occasionally like a shy child hiding behind its mother's skirts.

"Damn," Alex cursed, tripping over a clod of dirt and nearly plunging headfirst to the ground. It was so dark he could hardly see his hand in front of his face. He jumped as he heard a rustling movement in the tall grass to his left. Probably some nocturnal animal trying to find food. Alex picked up his pace, not wanting to encounter any night creatures.

When he reached the ridge, he paused a moment to look at Hannah's house. He could see its dark silhouette against the paler night sky, but the house radiated no lights, no life. Hannah and Edna must have already gone to bed.

He frowned as he thought of the older woman. He wanted to talk to Hannah, but he didn't want Edna's interference. Edna made her feeling for Alex quite obvious. He didn't want her influencing Hannah in any way.

He approached the dark house cautiously. Maybe he could sneak up to Hannah's bedroom window and they could talk without waking Edna. Yes, that seemed like the resourceful thing to do.

He moved to the side of the house, trying to discern which window might be Hannah's. One was completely closed, the heavy draperies pulled tightly shut. The other window was partially opened, the airy floral curtains moving gently with the influx of the cool night breeze. That had to be Hannah's. He could imagine her lying on pastel-colored sheets, the gentle wind stirring her nightgown, caressing her exposed skin. Yes, it had to be Hannah's window.

Alex softly eased the window up, hoping he could crawl in and awaken her quietly and not have to face the formidable Edna.

He'd managed to get his upper torso through the window when a piercing whistle resounded in his ear. He yelped in surprise, slamming the back of his head against the window frame. Before he had a chance to recover, his head was hit repeatedly with a pillow, the infernal whistling continuing shrilly. He knew in an instant what was happening—he'd chosen the wrong window.

Hannah sat up in bed, her heart racing frantically as she heard Edna's whistle piercing the silence of the night. In all the years Edna had worn the fool thing around her neck, Hannah had never heard it blown and she knew only something horrible would induce Edna to blow it.

Recognizing the potential danger of two women living alone, Hannah kept a baseball bat behind her bedroom door, and she grabbed it as she ran to Edna's room.

She paused in the doorway, aware of a skirmish taking place, but the room was too dark for her to see exactly what was happening. She fumbled along the wall for the light switch, flipped it on and stared in shock at the scene before her.

Edna stood, battle-wearied, her chest heaving with a bed pillow hefted over her head, ready to deliver a lethal blow. Alex was half in the room, effectively pinned by the half-closed window and the frame.

"Alex!" Hannah squeaked in surprise, setting the bat down on the floor and hurrying over to him. "What are you doing here?" She tried to pull the window up but found it stuck. "Edna, help me with this."

Reluctantly, Edna set her pillow down on the bed and approached them. "I don't know why I should help him. He near gave me a heart attack sneaking around like a thief in the night."

"I pity the thief who tries to break into this house," Alex retorted, feeling utterly ridiculous as the two women worked to raise the window.

"What are you doing here?" Hannah repeated as they got the window up and he crawled through and stood up.

"I wanted to talk to you," he answered.

"Haven't you ever heard of knocking on the front door?" Edna asked, reaching up to fix one of the pink foam curlers that had come undone in her hair.

Alex flushed, realizing now how stupid it had been for him to try to sneak in to talk to Hannah. "I'd really like to see you... alone."

"I don't think we have anything to say to each other," Hannah protested stiffly. She was irritated at him for just blundering in, not caring that the house was dark and they were already in bed. He'd thought only of his needs, only of the fact that he wanted to talk to her right now. The man was a textbook case of Arian traits.

"Hannah... please." The last word came with difficulty to his lips. He wasn't accustomed to having to humbly ask for anything. But, this was too important to let go. Hannah was becoming too important to let go.

"Either talk to him or don't talk to him, but whatever you decide to do, please don't do it in here," Edna said tiredly, crawling back into bed and glaring at both of them.

"Okay, let's go into the kitchen." Hannah relented, flipping off Edna's bedroom light and closing her door behind them.

They didn't speak until Alex was sitting at the kitchen table and Hannah was making a pot of coffee. "Hannah, I'm sorry..." Alex began with difficulty.

She turned and looked at him, a knowing smile on her face. "That's hard for you, isn't it? Apologizing."

He shrugged. "I don't have to do it very often." He studied her a moment, finding her intensely desirable with her hair tousled charmingly. She wore a cotton nightgown that was perfectly respectable, yet looked less so on her. The brushed cotton clung to her pert breasts, then fell gracefully to her ankles, and he knew the material would be soft beneath his fingers. He pulled his thoughts back to the matter at hand. "But, I also think you owe me an apology."

"For what?" She poured the water through the coffee machine then looked at him incredulously.

"For walking out on me, leaving behind some cryptic message that I assume was supposed to make me feel guilty."

"Did it make you feel guilty?" she asked.

Alex hesitated before answering. "Yes, it did," he admitted. "But it shouldn't have. Hannah, that was a legitimate business call. What did you expect? What did you want me to do?" His eyes darkened in frustration.

"I don't know what I expected," Hannah returned, her voice tense with an equal amount of frustration. "I only know that I promised myself this would never happen again. I would never get involved with a man who continually placed me on the back burner of his life." She began to pace back and forth in front of the table. "I've finished too many meals alone, attended too many parties because Edward chose business above all else." She stopped pacing and sat down across from him, her eyes beseeching him to understand her position.

"Alex, I can't go through a relationship like that again. Being married to Edward, living with his priorities, I became a shell of a human being, with no self-esteem, no sense of worth." She lowered her voice. "I walked out on you tonight because the whole scene was like a haunting from my past and I realized there can't be anything between the two of us."

Alex looked at her searchingly. At the moment, he couldn't imagine any man being fool enough to put her on a back burner. She looked so vulnerable, with her emotions in her eyes, remembered pain on her face. He wanted to take her into his arms and kiss away each hurt, ease all the heartache of her past.

He started to speak, but paused as she continued. "The whole problem is that you are an Aries and I'm a Cancer, and the two signs aren't very compatible. I should know—Edward was an Aries, too."

He looked at her in surprise. "You don't really believe in that astrological stuff, do you?"

Hannah shrugged. "I think there's an element of truth in it, and tonight proved that."

"It's not fair, you know," he said, reaching across the table to take one of her hands in his. She looked at him quizzically and he continued. "It's not fair that you're painting me with the same black brush as your ex-husband. It's not fair that you're blaming me for being born in the same month as Edward."

Hannah tried to pull her hand away, but he refused to relinquish his hold. "I can only judge you by what I've seen so far, and right now you're running true to Arian form."

"Hannah, I can't change my birthdate. Surely there is something redeeming about being an Arian."

Hannah flushed at his words. Of course he was right; there were a lot of admirable qualities in the Aries personality. They were optimistic and quick-witted. They had tremendous energy and enthusiasm. Was she being unreasonable in fearing a repeat of her marriage simply because the two men shared the same birth month?

Still, she was so afraid...afraid to trust him, frightened of being pulled back into a relationship that in the end would be destructive to her well-being. She studied the wooden tabletop in front of her, as if the answer would magically appear carved in the surface.

"Hannah." He spoke her name softly, and when she looked at him his eyes were warm, beckoning her to reconsider and she felt her firm resolve wavering, diminishing. "Compatible signs or not, you can't deny that there's something going on between us, some chemistry at work."

"Yes, but chemistry often causes dangerous explosions," she returned, wishing he would stop looking at her, stop making her remember the hunger, the desire he evoked in her.

He laughed at her answer, a low, seductive sound that made a small shiver race up her spine. "Oh, Hannah, don't turn your back on what's happening between us." His thumbs made tiny circles on the back of her hands. "Don't let your past intrude on your future." He looked into her eyes. "I can't promise you that I'm not going to make some mistakes. You know, this prioritizing thing is all new to me. And I can't promise you anything beyond each moment we spend together. But I don't want it to end like this, a decision made in the heat of the moment. I want to see where this...chemistry between us is going, don't you?"

"Yes," she whispered, unable to deny her own desire to follow through on whatever it was that existed between them. "Okay, Alex, I'll see it through, but we have to move slowly."

He squeezed her hands. "I'll move so slowly you'll think I'm going backward, if that's what you want."

"I don't know what I want," she finally confessed.

Alex nodded slowly, finding her words disturbing. He would have liked to believe that she wanted him, that all she needed was a little gentle prodding and tactful seduction and she would fall right into his arms. But, apparently it was not going to happen so easily.

Hannah was a perplexing enigma. In the past, Alex had found the combination of his good looks, wealth and power to be a sort of aphrodisiac on women, making relationships easy and fairly uncomplicated. But Hannah refused to follow in the pattern of his past, and again he found himself wondering what special magic it would take, what kind of key was needed to unlock the defenses that kept her wary of him.

"But you're right," she continued, her expression thoughtful. "There is something at work between us, and I'm not ready to walk away from it yet."

Alex expelled a tremendous sigh, not realizing how much he'd wanted her to come to that conclusion until this very moment. "Great," he exclaimed, realizing they'd just survived a crisis of sorts. "Now, are you going to pour me a cup of that coffee you made, or are you just going to continue to torture me by making me sit here and smell it?"

Hannah laughed, extricating her hands from his. "I'll pour you a cup on one condition...."

"What?"

"That you promise me you won't sneak into Edna's bedroom window anymore," she teased.

Alex groaned. "Please, don't remind me—the sound of that whistle is still reverberating in my ear and I'll never view a pillow quite in the same way again." He grinned, a smile that made him look like a mischievous boy. "I promise I'll never sneak into Edna's window again, but I'm making no promises where *your* window is concerned."

"Ah, if you think Edna wields a mean pillow, wait until you've met my baseball bat," she warned, then laughed at his look of disappointment. Still smiling, she poured him a cup of coffee.

The smile lingered on her face long after Alex had finished his coffee and left for home.

After rinsing out their cups, she grabbed a shawl and stepped out onto the front porch. The night enveloped her as she sat down on the stoop, pulling the shawl around her shoulders against the dark's cool breath.

Wise or foolish—she wasn't sure what category to place herself in. There seemed to be no middle ground where Alex was concerned, no gray areas where she could comfortably linger.

She felt as if by agreeing to continue to see him, she'd cast the dice. Now, she was powerless to stop the roll. She had to wait and see if the dice would turn a lucky seven, or end up craps.

If she'd been smart, she would have held on to the anger that had prompted her to leave him earlier in the evening. But that particular emotion had been difficult to maintain, first when he'd come crawling through the window, but more so later, as they'd sat together in the kitchen.

There had been something extremely intimate in the two of them sitting at the table sharing coffee and small talk while outside the world was sleeping. Yet it had been more than the intimacy of the scene that had finally made her capitulate and agree to continue seeing him. It had been the provocative warmth of his golden-brown eyes, the beckoning pressure of his hands on hers, the memory of his kisses that stirred her so deeply.

He'd been right—she couldn't deny there was something at work between them, and she couldn't deny her own desire to see it through. Foolish or wise... only time would tell.

"You seem preoccupied this morning. Is anything wrong?"

Hannah smiled at Alex's question, realizing that in the past week he had become more attuned to her moods. It had been five nights ago that they'd had their middle-of-the-night talk, and since then, they'd spent several hours together every day. The hours had been idyllic, time spent getting to know each other better, but true to his words, Alex was going slowly, not pressuring her with physical intimacy of any kind.

"Hannah?"

She flushed, realizing she hadn't answered him. "It's really no big deal." She frowned and plucked a piece of grass from the ground next to the blanket where they sat. "Edward called me yesterday. It seems one of my neighbors discovered he owns this property and they were pressuring him to get me off."

"Did he want you to move?" Alex asked, surprised at the panic that swept through him at the thought of no longer having her just over the ridge from his place.

"No, at least not yet." She grinned. "At least I should be grateful that Edward is stubborn and doesn't yield easily to pressure from anyone."

"You and Edward have remained friends despite the divorce?" Alex asked, again surprised at an alien emotion sweeping over him. Jealousy.

Hannah laughed and blew on the piece of grass, watching as it flew upward, then fluttered slowly back down to the ground. "I don't think my relationship with Edward could be considered a friendship, just a past acquaintance that reemerges sometimes due to necessity."

"Was your divorce painful?"

She paused a moment before answering, remembering that particular time in her life. "The divorce was necessary for my survival, but yes, it was painful. Failure always is."

She watched as Alex lay down on his back, his eyes focused thoughtfully on some distant point beyond the sky. "I sometimes wonder if my mother and father would have remained together if Mother hadn't died."

"Why do you say that?" Hannah asked curiously, stretching out beside him on her side. She stifled the impulse to reach out and run her hand through his hair, which was shining with burnished lights from the sun.

"I've just been thinking about my parents lately, and I've come to realize that they were very ill suited for each other."

"How so?" she asked, pleased that each day he had found it easier to talk about his parents, his mother in particular. It seemed he'd finally come to terms with his mother's death, and Hannah was grateful for the healing she sensed he'd accomplished.

"They were very different. My father was business-oriented, a workaholic who got his pleasure making money. My mother preferred the quiet life. She liked her music and gardening. She found pleasure in the simple things."

"That doesn't necessarily mean they would have divorced," Hannah observed. "Perhaps they had a compromise that worked for them."

He rolled onto his side so they were almost nose to nose. "And you and Edward couldn't find that compromise?"

She smiled. "With Edward there was no such thing as a compromise."

"Ah, his loss," Alex said, his tone as warm as the sun overhead. He reached out and touched her hair, as if overcome by the same impulse Hannah had been fighting. His eyes darkened and he leaned forward and she knew he was going to kiss her, and oh, how she wanted him to. At that moment, Edna yelled from the house.

"Hannah, that beast is loose again."

Hannah groaned and sat up, staring down at the rope that had held Sherman. Sure enough, the rope lay on the ground and there was no sign of the wayward animal. "I've got to go find him. I don't need any more neighbor trouble," she said reluctantly.

"I'll help you," Alex answered, standing up and holding out his hand to help her. She put her hand in his, and he pulled her up and against the length of him. Every nerve ending in her body screamed at the intimate contact, and an involuntary moan escaped her lips. "Alex." She quickly moved out of his embrace, knowing if she lingered there, she would never want to leave. "I have a sheep to catch."

"*We* have a sheep to catch," he corrected her, a smile on his face.

She liked the sound of that. *We*...so much nicer than *I*. In fact, as Alex grabbed her hand and they headed down the hill, she realized how much he had become part of her life over the past couple of days. She now anticipated seeing him the moment she awoke in the mornings, and he was the last thing she thought about when she went to sleep.

Sherman was found at the side of the house, contentedly munching the leaves off Edna's tomato plants. "Oh, Sherman, if Edna sees this, you're dead meat," Hannah exclaimed, tugging the sheep around the house and back to where Alex stood studying the rope.

"He chewed through it," Alex explained, holding up the frayed rope for her to see. "It looks like you need to find another way to contain the critter." He frowned, looking around the backyard. "Why can't you put him in with the horse? Surely they can't chew through a wooden fence."

"He can't, but there's a broken board over there." She pointed to the far side of the fence. "It makes a hole just big enough for Sherman to climb though."

"Then I'll just have to fix your fence," Alex observed, rolling up his shirtsleeves and rubbing his hands together.

"Oh, I can't let you do that," Hannah protested.

"Why not? Would you rather have Sherman run amuck and get you in trouble with your landlord?" When she didn't answer, he grinned. "Besides, you know how much men like to show off their prowess with tools. Just find me a hammer and some nails, and I'll be in macho heaven."

Hannah laughed. "Okay, you hold Sherman, and I'll get the tools." She waited until he had a firm grip on Sherman's leather collar, then she headed for the shed.

"If you keep running off and getting Hannah in trouble, I'm going to learn to like sheep stew," Alex growled at Sherman, who merely blinked in total disinterest.

As Hannah came back toward him, he realized again how beautiful she was, how much he had enjoyed the past couple of weeks. He'd been dreading his vacation until he'd met her. But the days had flown by in her company. It was strange really.... With other women he'd dated, he always made elaborate plans for the evenings, not wanting a moment of quiet time to pass between them. But with Hannah, he'd enjoyed simply being with her, sitting in silence or talking about their past and their future dreams. Being with her was enough and he felt no need for more. He now almost dreaded the fact that tomorrow he would be going back to work.

It was late evening by the time he realized he needed to go home and get things ready for his return to the work force the next day. They had mended the fence and Sherman was happily contained in the pen with Harriet the horse, and he and Hannah were sitting on the front porch watching the sun set.

"I'd better be getting home," he said, not moving from his position.

"Yes, and I have some notes to type up before tomorrow," she agreed, also not moving from her perch close to him. The sky in the west was an artist's palette of pinks and oranges, painting the entire twilight in watercolored hues. For a moment neither spoke, both enjoying the splendor in the sky.

"I go back to work tomorrow." The minute he said the words, the sun slipped beneath the horizon and the warmth disappeared, leaving behind paling colors that would eventually fade into a dismal grayness.

"Oh." Hannah tried to keep the disappointment out of her voice. Not yet—she wasn't ready to have this all end so soon.

"Hannah." He tipped her chin up and peered into her face. "I'm only going back to work, not moving to Africa."

"I know," she said, forcing a smile. Logically, she knew he had to return to his office, but she was afraid of what his going back to the corporate world would do to their relationship. Would she get lost in the shuffle of business deals and power lunches?

He kissed the end of her nose, and stood, pulling her up with him. "I don't know what my schedule will be tomorrow, with it being my first day back, but I'll call you."

She nodded. "Then I'll talk to you tomorrow."

"Tomorrow," he agreed, then he leaned down and kissed her. His lips were soft and warm against hers and Hannah wanted to melt against him and never let him go. But he released her almost immediately, smiling down at her. With a soft smile, he turned to leave.

As she watched him walk toward his house, she raised her hands to her lips, wanting to capture the feel of his mouth against hers forever. She had a horrible feeling that she might need the memory of his kiss to keep her warm in the night, because she didn't know if his going back to work would mean the beginning of the end for them.

Chapter Eight

Hannah waved as the car slowly pulled away from her house. It had been Christopher's last appointment with her and as always when she said goodbye to a patient, she felt a curious blend of emotions. There was the heady feeling of success mingled with the underlying sadness of the farewell.

Christopher was one of the lucky kids. Raised by a single, working mother, the twelve-year-old had fallen in with the wrong crowd and had begun to drink. Hannah had diagnosed the problem as the boy's bid for attention from a mother who was working two jobs to provide the tangibles for her son. Fortunately, the mother had taken Hannah's advice and had quit her evening job, devoting quality time to Christopher. That had been three months ago, and the turn-around in Chris had been nothing short of miraculous.

Hannah sighed and turned toward the house, un-surprised to see Edna standing on the front porch. "You okay?"

Hannah nodded and joined her. "Chris and his mother are going to be just fine."

"But what about you?" Edna eyed her critically. "You haven't been sleeping well, and you aren't eat-ing enough to keep a bird alive."

"I'm all right. I've just been restless, that's all." Hannah sat down on the porch stoop.

"It's this neighbor thing, isn't it?" Edna asked, groaning as she plopped down next to Hannah.

"It's just a worry. I can't help but be on edge. Ed-ward has phoned twice in the past week to complain about calls he's getting. I was hoping that now that Sherman can't escape and is no longer a nuisance, the neighbors would ease up. I don't know how much longer Edward is going to let me stay here."

"He has to let you stay," Edna protested indig-nantly. "When you got divorced, he promised you could stay here as long as you wanted."

Hannah smiled tightly. "Yes, but it wasn't part of the divorce agreement. It was just a verbal promise, and we both know what Edward's promises are worth."

For a long moment the two women were silent, staring out over the place they had both come to con-sider home.

"I'm too old to move," Edna said, breaking the silence and swatting at a fly that tormented her hair. "Couldn't you talk to Alex about helping?"

Hannah looked at Edna in amazement, then grinned. "You mean, ask the devil himself for help?"

Edna flushed lightly. "Oh, he's not so bad. He can't be all bad if Jacob has been working for him all these years."

"That reminds me, I've been meaning to ask you about Jacob." Hannah looked at the older woman slyly. "You've been seeing an awful lot of him lately. Am I going to have to find myself a new housekeeper?"

"Don't be ridiculous," Edna scoffed, her face reddening to the color of an overripe tomato. "I've just been helping him rearrange the kitchen. I've never known a man who had any sense when it comes to setting up kitchen cabinets. Jacob may know the proper way to be a valet, he might know the proper way to introduce people and chauffeur, but he doesn't know beans about having a good time."

"Ah, it's nice that you're taking such an interest in a neighbor," Hannah mused indulgently.

"Well, don't be hiring my replacement," Edna snapped, rising up from the porch. "I'm just being nice to the old man. There's no reason to make such a big deal out of it." She glared at Hannah. "And talk to Alex. Maybe he can help with this neighbor situation." With that, she stomped inside.

Hannah stifled a giggle with her hand. Yes, there was definitely something at work between Edna and

Jacob. Edna could deny it until she was blue in the face, but Hannah had seen the way the two looked at each other. Hannah's smile slowly faded as she thought of Edna's last words. "'Talk to Alex,'" she muttered. Wouldn't she love to? It had been two days since she'd last heard from him.

He'd called her Monday, Tuesday and Wednesday—short calls from his office. But since Wednesday, there had been nothing. Hannah knew it was as much this as the neighbor thing that was causing her sleepless nights. She missed him. She missed his presence in her life. The past three days had seemed empty and lifeless, endlessly long.

It had become apparent to her that Alex had fallen right back into his old work habits and patterns. Their relationship had been placed in the back of his mind with work at the forefront. It saddened her. She'd felt they were building something real, something of value, but apparently she'd been mistaken. It was as she had initially feared—she had been a pleasant interlude, a stimulating way for him to pass his vacation. But now, he was back in his real world, and there was no room for her. With a sigh, Hannah rose, deciding she needed to feed her animals, get her mind off Alex.

It was nearly noon when Edna stuck her head out the door and yelled to Hannah that she had a phone call.

Hannah hurried inside, picked up the receiver. "Hello?"

"I was sitting here at my desk on the fourteenth floor and outside my window in the clouds I saw a unicorn dancing on a rainbow."

Hannah closed her eyes in relief and squeezed the phone more tightly against her ear. Alex's voice was like a balm soothing a wound, a reassurance that she wasn't forgotten. She grinned. "When you start seeing pink elephants I suggest you head to a doctor and get that fixed," she teased.

Alex laughed. "I've missed our cloud watching," he said, the softness of his tone caressing the receiver. "It's not much fun without you."

"That's nice to hear. I was beginning to wonder if you were finding your figures and deals much more exciting than being with me." Her voice held a touch of censure. "I'm sorry," she added contritely. "I didn't mean for it to sound that way."

"No, it's all right. I owe you an apology," he quickly interjected. "I've been meaning to call you for the past couple of days, but things have been a little crazy around here. If you want chaos, just let the boss be away for a couple of weeks." Actually, it was more than this. The past couple of days had been a revelation to Alex, but he wasn't ready to tell Hannah this—not yet. "I'm going to compound my sin by asking you to an impromptu gathering tonight."

"What sort of gathering?" she asked.

"It's a business meeting disguised as a cocktail party. It's being held here, in the lobby of my office building, and the guest of honor is Max Wilding."

"Oh, Alex, I don't think..."

"Hannah, I'd really like for you to be here with me."

"I haven't been to a cocktail party for years," she said, her reluctance obvious across the lines. "They are one of the things I gave up with my divorce."

"I know it's short notice, and I know it's not the kind of thing you like to do, but, Hannah, I'd really like for you to come."

"I... All right," she conceded.

"Great," Alex replied with exuberance. "I'll have Jacob pick you up about six and bring you into the city. We can make the rest of the arrangements once you're here. I'll see you tonight." Before she had a chance to change her mind, he hung up. With a smile of contentment he stared out the window, absently watching the clouds skittering by.

Actually, he hadn't been completely truthful with her. The cocktail party had been set up two days ago, when his negotiations with Max Wilding had been completed. The minute he'd arranged things for the party, he'd thought about his usual escort for such events—Miranda. But when he'd thought of her, it had been with the realization that he didn't want to see her anymore. When the announcement was made to the press this evening, detailing the Wilding deal, he wanted Hannah by his side.

When he'd decided he didn't want to see Miranda again, he'd called her and made plans to meet her for lunch. Over a meal at the Plaza yesterday, he had told her he wasn't going to see her anymore. Miranda had accepted his decision with her usual passionless graciousness, the flaring of her nostrils the only indication that she was miffed.

Alex wasn't worried about Miranda. She was a survivor, and he knew he hadn't been her only eligible escort in the months they'd been dating.

His contented smile stretched bigger as he thought of the evening to come. Wouldn't Hannah be surprised when she learned the outcome of the Wilding deal? His smile grew thoughtful. Wasn't it strange that he'd spent most of his life trying to please his distant, hard-to-reach father, and after his father's death, Alex had worked hard at pleasing nobody but himself. Now, it suddenly seemed eminently important that he please Hannah. What, exactly, did it all mean?

He jumped as his secretary buzzed to let him know his two o'clock appointment had arrived.

"I can't believe I agreed to this. I can't go. I have nothing suitable to wear." Hannah stood in front of her closet clad in her slip and panty hose, her eyes frantic with near-hysteria.

Edna calmly moved her aside and fumbled at the back of the closet. "What about this?" she asked, pulling out a pink, frilly dress.

"No, that's all wrong. It was a mistake when I bought it and five years of hanging in my closet hasn't changed that fact." Hannah sank down on her bed, trying to fight the waves of panic that had been sweeping over her ever since she'd agreed to go to the cocktail party. "I should have told him no. I should have absolutely refused to go."

"So, why didn't you?" Edna asked, her head still buried in the closet.

"Because it was so obvious he wanted me to go," Hannah answered softly. She hadn't been able to refuse him, not when his voice had been so invoking. Besides, she had suddenly realized that if she wanted things to work out between the two of them, she was going to have to try to keep up with him, let him know what was important to him was also important to her.

Edna peered out of the closet, looking at Hannah critically. "I knew it—I knew you'd do something stupid like fall in love with him."

Hannah opened her mouth to protest, then snapped it shut in astonishment. In love with Alex? Impossible, wasn't it? And yet, she had to consider the possibility. Why else had she agreed to go with him tonight, when she absolutely abhorred cocktail parties and the surface talk and plastic smiles that went along with them?

"Didn't you have a little black dress? A silk one with a bit of a flared skirt?" Edna disappeared back into the dark recesses of the closet and Hannah continued to consider her own unsettling thoughts.

In love with Alex... heaven help her, but she didn't want to be. Edna had warned her over and over again about the dangers of a Cancer falling in love with an Aries, and Hannah had her past experiences to reinforce this to her. Alex was a poor bet for a long-term relationship. So why was she going tonight? It didn't matter, she decided, refusing to explore her innermost feelings any further. It was a matter of friendship, a token of affection, but it was definitely not a sign of love. No way was she going to be foolish enough to fall in love with a man like Alexander Donaldson III.

Hannah stood in the corner of the lavish lobby of the office building, trying to stifle her impulse to hide behind the large, artificial palm tree that stood next to her.

Jacob had dropped her off nearly twenty minutes before and as yet she had seen no sign of Alex.

She was grateful that the black dress Edna had encouraged her to wear fit right in with the evening attire and didn't appear as dated as it was. She wouldn't want to embarrass Alex by being inappropriately dressed.

"Ah, another escapee from the insane asylum trying to hide behind the fake foliage."

Hannah jumped at the deep voice coming from the other side of the palm tree. Peering around a frond, she saw a big, burly man sitting on a chair that had been pulled behind the plant. "I much prefer to enjoy these sort of gatherings from a distant vantage point."

Hannah returned his smile. "I agree. I'm only here because someone specifically asked me to be."

"Hmm, me, too." He shook his head and pulled on his grizzled gray beard. "It's amazing what we put ourselves through to please other people."

"Yes, isn't it?" Hannah said thoughtfully. Strange, she hadn't put herself out for anybody in a very long time. She'd tried so hard to make Edward happy, had given so much of herself, that when she'd finally gotten away from him she'd wallowed in selfishness, pleasing nobody but herself. It felt good to be here now, knowing she was here because Alex wanted her to be here. It felt good to be giving again.

"I never did go in much for these fancy, dancy parties. I'd rather be fiddling around in my shed."

Hannah, remembering everything Alex had told her about the eccentric Max Wilding, suddenly realized to whom she was talking. "Mr. Wilding, could I get you a glass of champagne?" she asked.

His blue eyes lit up. "Yes...yes that would be quite nice. Of course, I'd much prefer a double Scotch on the rocks, but a bit of champagne will do."

Spying a waiter carrying a tray of filled champagne glasses, Hannah slipped out of the corner, grabbed two of the drinks, then returned to her original position. She handed Max one, then took a sip of her own. Perhaps a glass of champagne would steel her nerves, chase away the fluttering in the pit of her stomach.

"What's a pretty young woman like you doing hiding out here in the corner?" Max's blue eyes peered at her quizzically, his bushy white eyebrows dancing upward.

"It's been a long time since I've been to a cocktail party," Hannah explained. "I guess I just feel a little bit out of sync."

"Oh, well it shouldn't take you long to get back into the swing of things. Most young woman love these sort of gatherings."

Hannah considered this thoughtfully. Yes, there had been a time when she had enjoyed cocktail parties and theater outings. Perhaps when she'd divorced Edward and isolated herself, she'd taken it one step too far, isolating herself from life itself. Before she had a chance to delve further into these thoughts, Max spoke again.

"Well, it looks like our host has finally arrived."

Hannah's gaze followed Max's and she saw Alex standing on the bottom step of the wide staircase that led to the upstairs offices. It had been almost a week since she'd last seen him, and her heart jumped into her throat as she looked at him. She'd forgotten how achingly handsome he was. He was dressed impeccably in a black tuxedo, the formal wear looking as if it had been made just for him. He looked coolly detached, firmly in control, the master of all he surveyed.

Then he spied her across the room, and the cool detachment on his features melted, giving way to a look of such warmth, a smile of such pleasure that Hannah felt a languid heat race through her veins. It was at that moment, with him making his way through the crowd to her, that Hannah knew, Aries or not, she was hopelessly in love with Alex Donaldson.

Chapter Nine

"I'm ready to get out of here. How about you?" Alex breathed into Hannah's ear.

The gathering was winding down. The announcements had been made to the press and the crowd had thinned to a handful of stalwart partiers.

Hannah smiled up at him and nodded. She was exhausted and they still had an hour's drive ahead of them to get back to their homes on Long Island.

"Come on." He placed his arm lightly around her shoulders and led her over to the elevators, where he pushed the Down button. "Have I told you tonight that you look lovely?" he asked as they waited for the elevator to arrive.

"Several times, but don't let that stop you from telling me again," Hannah teased, stepping through the door as it swooshed open. Alex followed her and as the doors closed, he pulled her into his arms.

"May I say you look beautiful tonight, Ms. Martinof."

"Thank you, Mr. Donaldson. You're looking quite dashing yourself." Hannah smiled, feeling a tinge of sudden shyness as she studied his strong, handsome face. She loved him, but the knowledge of her love was still too new for her to feel comfortable with it.

"You seemed to have a good time tonight," he observed.

She nodded and moved out of his arms as the elevator began to descend. "I had a wonderful time. I'd forgotten how nice it can be to mingle with people, enjoy social conversation. I particularly enjoyed talking to Max Wilding."

"He's a rough old codger, isn't he?" Alex said, leading her out of the elevator and into an underground parking lot. "That business was Max Wilding's life. What did you think of the announcement to the press? Were you surprised?"

"A little. When did you decide not to buy Wilding Electronics?" As they walked, Hannah remembered how when the announcement had been made to the press detailing that the Donaldson Corporation had not bought, but had rather merely invested in Wilding Electronics, Alex had been watching her. His face had reflected boyish anticipation as he observed her reaction.

"Remember the conversation we had when we first met, about me not really needing another company to run?" He continued when she nodded. "I guess some of it sank in, made sense."

"So you decided to invest instead of buy, and let Max continue to run the company." Hannah stifled a yawn with the back of her hand. "Sorry," she said, smiling crookedly. "I'm not used to party hours."

"Actually, I'm exhausted myself," he admitted as they reached his sports car. "It's been a long week for me." He opened the passenger door. "I've got an apartment not far from here. We could go there and spend the night, then make the long drive home in the morning when we're fresh."

"Oh... I couldn't do that... Edna would worry if I didn't show up tonight."

"Hannah, my apartment has a phone. You could call her and let her know we're staying here for the night."

"But... I... don't have any pajamas or anything."

He smiled at her indulgently. "I'm sure I could manage to dig out a spare pair of pj's for you."

She hesitated, unsure exactly what it was that Alex was asking her.

"It's a two-bedroom apartment," he added, as if guessing what she was thinking. "I'll be glad to take you home tonight if that's what you want."

Hannah looked at him, noting the lines of fatigue that radiated outward from his eyes. He did look tired, and she had to admit, the thought of a nearby bed was vastly appealing, far more so than a long drive. "I suppose I could call Edna," she said thoughtfully.

"Thanks. I was dreading the trip home tonight." Alex took her hand and pulled it to his lips, placing a kiss in its palm. As always, at his touch, Hannah felt heat suffuse her body and she wondered what it would be like to make love with him. She got into the car, her thoughts still treading dangerous ground. He would be an excellent lover, and she now realized the depths of her feelings for him, but was she ready to make a final commitment to him and physically express her love? She wasn't sure. She had no idea how he felt about her. If he made a move tonight when they were alone together in his apartment, she didn't know what her reaction would be. But she had a feeling it wouldn't take much of a push from him to get her into his bed.

Alex closed the passenger door, then walked around the car to the driver's side, a whistle jumping to his lips. He was more excited than he could remember being in a very long time. And he knew the excitement was being generated by the thought of spending the night in his apartment with Hannah. He'd told her the apartment had two bedrooms, but he was hoping that tonight, only one would be necessary.

As he started the car, he turned the radio to a station playing soft, relaxing music. It filled the car, making conversation unnecessary. They drove in silence, Alex focused on the heavy traffic that, even at this late hour, clogged the streets. While he concentrated on his driving skills, Hannah studied him.

Even with the lines of his face deepened by fatigue, there was still an aura of strength and pride to his features. Hannah had a feeling that the woman who captured him would be the luckiest woman in the whole world. If Alex ever gave his heart, she knew he would bring to that relationship the same passion, the same intensity he brought to each of his business deals. This thought made her shiver involuntarily.

"Cold?" He looked over at her and smiled, a smile with enough warmth to cause a fire to ignite deep in the pit of her stomach.

"No, I'm fine," she answered, feeling the flame inside her surge hotter as he reached one hand out and placed it on her thigh. His touch was not improper, making small circles on the material of her dress just above her knee. But it was as powerful as a caress to her breast, or a kiss on the back of her neck, causing the heat inside her to liquefy to a river of boiling lava.

She wasn't sure whether she was disappointed or relieved when he removed his hand to downshift and turn the car into a parking garage.

From the garage they got into an elevator that whisked them up to the top floor.

"The penthouse?" she mused as they stepped into a lush, carpeted foyer with a single apartment door before them.

"I know you too well to think you're impressed," Alex said with a smile as he opened the door and ushered her inside.

He was wrong. Hannah couldn't help but be impressed. The apartment floor was covered in a white, thick carpet that half swallowed her shoes as she moved across the room, drawn to a wall of windows that led to a balcony. "May I?" she asked, her hand reaching for the handle of the French doors.

"Allow me." He opened the doors and followed her as she stepped out onto the balcony.

The warm summer night breeze caressed her face and arms as she walked over to the ledge, peering out into the distance. Below them was the East River, filling the air with its pungent damp scent, and across, on the other side of the river, the distant lights of Queens lit up the sky.

"It's beautiful out here," Hannah murmured softly. They were up high enough so that the city noises were muted, like a dream half-remembered. She looked upward and saw that her ruling planet, the moon, was full and brilliant. It only added to the magic of the night, making her feel intoxicated by its illumination.

Alex placed an arm around her shoulders, pulling her close against his side. "It is beautiful, isn't it?" he agreed. "I have a confession to make... I've owned this apartment for almost a year, and I've never stood on this balcony before tonight."

Hannah looked up at him in surprise. "Why not?"

Alex shrugged. "I don't stay here very often. This apartment is usually used for business acquaintances who fly into town to deal with the Donaldson Corporation. I stay here only when I'm too tired to go home, and usually on those nights, I come in and go right to bed."

"Such a shame," Hannah said ruefully. "You miss an awful lot of life being too busy or too tired."

"I realize just how much I've missed every time I'm with you," he replied, and he pulled her around to stand in front of him. Hannah knew he was going to kiss her—his intentions were clearly on his face, and she raised her lips to give him easier access.

She tasted of pale pink lipstick and champagne and womanly warmth, and Alex immediately felt himself responding to her. Never had he been so patient in pursuing a woman, but now his patience was wearing thin. He wanted this woman he held in his arms, and never had the time seemed so right as it did at this very moment. He deepened the kiss, wanting to inhale her very essence within, capture it for future memories. He reached up and tangled his fingers in her short, silken hair, leaning into her to make her aware of his arousal. She sighed against his mouth, wrapping her arms around his waist and fitting her soft curves to his firm physique.

Alex had never wanted a woman more, and he tried to communicate his want—his need—for her in his kiss, his caress. But he didn't want her out here on the balcony. He wanted her in his bed, beneath the cool whisper of sheets where he could explore the secret mysteries of her body at leisure. Reluctantly, he released his hold on her, stepping back and looking at her face, noting how the moonlight loved her features. Her eyes were dazed, as if she were just awakening from a dream.

"Hannah." He whispered her name and took her hand, leading her back inside.

Hannah felt as if she'd just surfaced in a pool of murky water. The maelstrom of emotions that had kept her reservations silent suddenly departed, making her aware of the promises her kisses had made, promises her good sense demanded be broken.

"Alex," she said regretfully as he attempted to pull her into his arms once again. She could tell by the look on his face, the fire in his eyes, that he had interpreted her kisses as acquiescence. "I'm really tired. All I need at the moment is to go to bed."

"My sentiments exactly," Alex said with a smile that let Hannah know he had completely misunderstood her statement.

"Alex . . ." She looked at him awkwardly, watching the smile on his face flicker, then fade. "I apologize. Out there on the balcony, I lost touch with reality for a moment. But the reality is that I'm not ready for you and me to . . ." She saw the muscles working in his jawline, read the irritation that darkened his eyes.

"Fine," he said tersely, making her wonder if she'd blown everything that might have been between them. "I'll show you to your room."

As she followed behind him, her heart ached and regret weighed heavily. Had she made a mistake? Should she have put her reservations aside and made love with him?

He flipped on a light in a large bedroom with modern, impersonal furnishings. "You'll find pajamas in the bottom drawer and help yourself to anything you need in the bathroom. I'll see you in the morning."

With these curt words, Alex disappeared back into the living room, leaving her to stare after him.

She closed the bedroom door and found the pajamas where he said they would be. As she changed into them, her mind whirled with self-recriminations. She was a fool to deny herself the pleasure of making love with him. They were both adults, and she had a feeling Alex was not the kind of man who would endlessly wait for any woman. It was quite possible that tonight would be the end for the two of them.

She went into the adjoining bathroom and washed her face, then shut off the bedroom light and crawled into bed. Her lips felt swollen and wanting from the intensity of the kisses they had shared on the balcony. She ran her finger over her lips thoughtfully. Had she made a mistake? Somehow, despite her reservations, she didn't think so. She was certain of her feelings concerning Alex. She loved him, and in making love with him, she knew her heart would be irrevocably committed. But what about him? How did he feel about her? She knew she fascinated him, amused him, but that was a long way from love.

No, she hadn't made a mistake. It was right that she had told Alex no. The only thing that could induce her to pursue a physical relationship with him was love, and so far that was a commodity Alex wasn't offering.

Alex stepped out onto the balcony, wishing he still smoked and had a cigarette to puff away some of his frustration. Frustration... God, that didn't even begin to describe what he was feeling at the moment. Irritation, aggravation and more than a little bit of good old-fashioned anger. And it was all directed at the woman who was sleeping in the bedroom.

He leaned against the railing, staring out into the distance, trying to figure out Hannah Martinof. She was a puzzle he couldn't discern, a deal he couldn't close. What did she want from him? He'd tried subtle seduction, he'd tried endless patience. She'd wanted him. He knew with a certainty that she had been ready to capitulate while they were out on the balcony. She'd returned his kisses with a hunger that made him ache for more. What he should do right now, he told himself, is march right into that bedroom and take her.

He sighed and ran a hand through his hair. He knew he wouldn't do that. He didn't want Hannah that way. He didn't want to have to talk her into making love with him. He wanted her to come willingly, eagerly into his arms. So, what did it take to get her to that point?

He breathed deeply of the night air, noting the stars overhead. It was a beautiful night. Funny, he wouldn't have noticed that before meeting Hannah. She had brought a new perspective to his life. He felt his frustration slowly ebbing away. He'd never worked so hard, or waited so long for a woman, but he had the feeling that Hannah was worth the wait.

"Good morning," he greeted Hannah brightly as she came out of the bedroom early the next day.

"Morning," she returned tentatively, self-consciously smoothing down the skirt of her black dress.

"I hope you slept well."

She nodded, eyeing him curiously. She'd expected irritation, silence and male pouting, but he looked as if nothing was wrong and the night before hadn't happened.

"Would you like some coffee or something, or shall we just go ahead and take off for home?"

"We'd better head home," Hannah replied with a small grimace. "I forgot to call Edna last night and she's probably got the National Guard out looking for me."

"I imagine Jacob told her that I planned to spend the night here," Alex said, then grinned at her. "Yes, I told Jacob we would be staying here."

"You were terribly sure of yourself," Hannah replied with a frown.

Alex shrugged. "You can't blame a guy for trying."

Hannah smiled. "No, I guess I can't. Alex, about last night..."

He held up his hands to still her words. "Hannah, I'm not going to pretend that I wasn't disappointed. I'd hoped for different sleeping arrangements last night. I want you, and I'm not a man who gives up easily."

Hannah felt a warm blush color her cheeks. "And I have to do what I think is right for me...for us. Last night just didn't feel right."

He reached out and took her hands in his. "I understand that. I want you to understand that I'm not going to give up. I can be relentless when it comes to achieving what I want."

"Alex, I'm not a company waiting to be taken over, and I'm not a share of stocks needing to be bought. You seem to couch everything in terms that sound like business deals," she chided him.

He laughed. "Come on, let's go home, and on the drive we can discuss the negotiations of this particular 'deal.'"

Moments later, as they were driving across the Queensboro Bridge, Hannah asked, "Have you always gotten what you wanted?"

"Sure," he answered flippantly. "Well, actually, that's not exactly true. I wanted to be a Boy Scout and I never got a chance."

"Really?"

He nodded. "I had a friend who was a Scout, and he and his dad were always doing these wonderful things, going camping together, building wooden race cars, hiking and collecting leaves off trees." He frowned. "It took me a month to get up my nerve to ask my father if I could join, if it wasn't something we could do together. He laughed at the very idea, said that if I wanted to do something with him, I could spend time at his office learning the business. I was eight years old, for God's sakes."

There was a touch of bitterness in his voice, an echo of past unfulfillment that strummed an answering chord in Hannah. All too vividly she could imagine him as a little boy, desperately wanting, needing his father's attention, only to be taught that business came first. She reached over and lightly touched his hand. "You would have made a wonderful Boy Scout."

"Thanks," he said, smiling at her with pleasure.

The harmony between them continued until they pulled up in front of Hannah's place. "Thank you, Alex, for a wonderful evening."

"I could have made it even more wonderful," he replied.

"I'm sure you could have," she agreed, getting out of the car.

"Picnic tomorrow?" he asked.

"Sounds great. How about around noon?"

"I'll see you then." She watched as he pulled down the driveway, the car eventually disappearing in a cloud of dust.

"Well, I guess Sherman isn't the only wayward creature around these parts."

Hannah turned around to see Edna standing on the porch, her arms folded rigidly across her ample chest and her eyebrows meeting over her nose in disapproval.

"Oh, Edna, I'm sorry I didn't call you last night to let you know about our plans to stay in the city."

"Hmm, no need to apologize to me." Edna sniffed with indignation. "I'm just the housekeeper around here. Besides, Jacob told me of your plans. *He* didn't want me staying awake and worrying about you."

Hannah approached the older woman and placed an arm around her. "Edna, you know that you're much more than a housekeeper. And I do owe you an apology. You're my friend, and I should have called."

Edna looked slightly mollified. "I imagine you had more important things on your mind last night," she said, letting Hannah know she was still miffed.

"Edna, if it eases your mind at all, my virtue is untainted. Alex's apartment is a two-bedroom, and both were slept in last night."

Edna's features relaxed in visible relief. "Oh, honey, I can't help it. I just worry about you."

Hannah kissed her plump cheek. "That's why I love you," she exclaimed, moving past Edna to go into the house.

"You love too easily," Edna retorted, following in Hannah's footsteps. "I just want to make sure you aren't making a mistake with Alex. He seems to be so much like Edward."

"But he isn't. Not really," Hannah protested, sinking down on the sofa while Edna sat in the chair across from her. "Oh, I have to admit, at first I thought Alex was nothing but an Edward clone. And Alex does possess all of the Arian traits that destroyed my first marriage, but they are tempered with so many wonderful traits." She leaned forward, eager to tell Edna what she felt about Alex. "Edna, Alex is a good man. He's just forgotten how to be human rather than some businessman robot. But, I see him changing all the time, rediscovering himself and a whole new world."

"You can't count on a man changing just to please a woman," Edna scoffed.

"Alex isn't changing to please me," Hannah said thoughtfully. "In fact, I don't think he's changing so much as simply regressing, becoming the man he might have been had his mother lived."

"I hope you're right, honey. But it's been my experience that a man can't change what the stars demand he be. And Alexander Donaldson is an Aries, and he'll break your heart just like Edward." With this pronouncement, Edna got up and disappeared into the kitchen.

Chapter Ten

"Hannah...wake up. The animals are gone."

Edna's urgent voice penetrated Hannah's deep sleep. Hannah groaned at the interruption of her pleasant dreams, Edna's words not yet penetrating through the fog.

"I'll feed them later," she mumbled, burrowing deeper beneath the sheet.

"Hannah, you can't feed them. They aren't there."

"What?" Hannah sat up, rubbing her hands over her eyes in an effort to wake up. She looked over at her alarm clock, shocked to see it was almost nine o'clock. She couldn't remember the last time she'd slept so late. She turned her gaze back to Edna, who stood next to the bed, twisting a dish towel into an unrecognizable form.

"I went outside on the porch to shake out a few throw rugs, and Sherman and Harriet aren't in the pen."

Hannah's sleep-fogged brain cleared and she jumped out of bed. Pulling on her robe, she flew out of the house and onto the porch. Sure enough, the wooden pen was empty. There was no sign of the sheep or the horse.

"Oh, Sherman, how did you manage this?" Hannah murmured as she ran toward the pen, her gaze darting left and right, searching for a glimpse of the missing creatures.

She wasn't overly concerned, knowing that both animals would return home when they got hungry or tired. However, she was worried about the trouble either animal could cause with her neighbors.

She stared at the heavy latch on the wooden gate. How on earth had Sherman managed to push the latch to the unlock position, then open the burdensome gate? He couldn't, she decided with a sinking heart. Sherman could eat a flower bed to stubbles in seconds, he could trample a garden with ease, but there was no way he could unlock a gate and push it open. It would take a human hand to accomplish this task. Probably the same hands that had taken such pleasure in painting her shed.

She looked at the rabbit hutch and moaned in distress. The door to the hutch hung open and there wasn't a single furry bunny in sight. Even Rocky the raccoon, who rarely left the tree he called home, was nowhere to be seen.

"Damn them," she muttered, her eyes filling with tears of frustration. Why were they doing this to her? Why this personal vendetta against her? And how could she fight an enemy she never saw, one who attacked in the darkness of night?

"Hannah?" Edna came up behind her and placed a comforting hand on her shoulder.

"Oh, Edna," Hannah sighed, trying to keep the tremble out of her voice, knowing how emotional the older woman became when Hannah was upset. "Somebody let them all go, and they must have scared them, because none of the animals are anywhere around."

"They'll all come back home," Edna said in an effort to soothe her.

"Perhaps, but where does all this stop?" She turned around to face Edna. "How many more times am I going to have to repaint the shed, or round up the animals? With things like this happening, how much longer is Edward going to let us remain here?" In frustration, Hannah raced a hand through her sleep-tousled hair. "Maybe it would be best if I started looking for someplace else to live. Perhaps someplace in upstate New York, or Connecticut."

"So, they win and you give up?" Edna looked at her disapprovingly. "What about all your patients who depend on you? Are you just going to abandon them? What about little Carrie, who you've said is on the verge of a breakthrough? Can you just move away and leave her in her own little world of misery?"

"Carrie." Hannah's eyes widened. "Edna, what time is it?"

"Almost nine-thirty. Why?"

"Carrie has an eleven o'clock appointment. She loves Peter Rabbit. What's she going to do if she arrives here and Peter is gone?" Hannah felt the beginnings of panic stir inside her. "Oh, Edna, it might throw her right back where she was when she first started seeing me. We've got to find that rabbit before she gets here."

"You go and get dressed," Edna instructed firmly, as always at her best in the midst of a crisis. "While you're doing that I'll search around the hutch area, then together we'll spread out until we find him."

Hannah nodded and ran quickly to the house. As she dressed, she thought of all the places the animals might have gone. Sherman had probably headed over to Alex's, where new flower beds had been planted. The horse might have gone the same way, finding Alex's lush lawn a temptation too difficult to ignore. The rabbits would be the most difficult to find. Her heart skipped a beat as a sudden thought crossed her mind. Surely the people who'd released them wouldn't have taken the rabbits, or harmed them in any way. Surely they hadn't been that cruel.

She was just about to fly back outside when the ringing of the phone stopped her. She grabbed up the receiver, her turmoil evident in her abrupt greeting. "Yes?"

"Hannah? Is that you?"

"Oh, Alex, I can't talk right now. We have an emergency here. Somebody let all the livestock loose, and Carrie's coming for her appointment at eleven and if we don't find Peter I don't know what Carrie will do." The words tumbled out of her in a rush of despair.

"Hannah, honey, slow down. I can't make sense of what you're saying," Alex instructed her. Again, she explained to him what had happened, slower this time. "What time is Carrie's appointment?" he asked when she had finished speaking.

"Eleven."

"Okay, you keep looking and I'll be there to help as soon as I can. If I push it, I can be there in forty-five minutes."

"Oh, Alex, you're at work. I can't let you do that," Hannah protested, warmed merely by his offer. "There's really nothing you can do."

"I can help you look, and I can give you a hug. You sound like you could use one." There was a long pause. "Hannah, are you still there?"

"Yes, I'm here," she replied, once again feeling the sting of hot tears burning at her eyes. "And yes, I could use a hug."

"I'll be there as soon as I can." Alex hung up the phone, thinking about the meeting he was supposed to be holding in thirty minutes. It was an important one with his lawyer and a representative from the labor union. One of his plant's labor forces was threatening a strike. Even as he contemplated the repercussions of postponing the meeting, his mind replayed his conversation with Hannah. She'd been unable to disguise her despair and he knew no matter what the repercussions, he was going to miss that meeting. He punched his intercom button. "Anne, cancel my conference with Tom Richards and Mr. Watson and have the garage bring my car around. I've got an emergency at home."

"Yes, sir," his secretary replied, her voice reflecting a touch of astonishment.

Within minutes, Alex was in his car, whizzing toward Long Island and Hannah. It was no wonder Anne had looked at him strangely as he'd left. He couldn't remember ever leaving his office in the middle of the morning. For most of his work life, Alex had always been the first to arrive in the mornings and the last one to leave at night. Strange—he'd half expected to feel guilty as he walked out and got into his car. But instead of guilt, he had been surprised to feel a rightness in his gut. Hannah needed him, and never in his life had Alex realized how wonderful it was to be needed.

Hannah had brought a new dimension to his life, and one of these days he was going to have to figure out exactly where the two of them were headed. She cared about him—he was certain of that. But there was a piece of herself she refused to relinquish to him. It was more than the fact that she wasn't ready to make love with him. There was a piece of her heart that she guarded closely, and he wondered what it would take, what he had to do to attain that particular part of her.

It took him exactly forty-two minutes to arrive and the first thing he saw was Edna and Hannah sitting on the front porch. Harriet and Sherman were back in their pen, but Alex could tell by the look on Hannah's face that Peter hadn't been found.

As he got out of the car, Hannah left the porch to meet him. Without saying a word, he opened his arms and she moved into his embrace as if it was where she belonged. For a long moment he merely held her, not speaking, hoping his arms were communicating what she most needed to hear.

Eventually, she stepped back from him and he cupped her face in his hands, peering into her green eyes, eyes that reflected her pain, her hurt and frustration. "Are you okay?" he asked.

She nodded slowly. "We found them all except two rabbits. We can't find Peter, and Carrie should be here in just a few minutes."

"What exactly happened?"

Hannah shrugged, leading him up to the porch where Edna was standing. "Sometime last night or early this morning, somebody released them all."

"And I'd be willing to gamble my whistle that it was the same two rotten kids who love to leave their artistic markings all over the shed," Edna exclaimed fervently.

"Hannah, this has all gotten out of control. Something is going to have to be done," Alex said.

Hannah shrugged again—a gesture that spoke of her helplessness. "I don't know what to do. I don't know how to fight this."

"We'll think of something." Alex's voice was reassuring as he placed an arm around her shoulder.

Hannah leaned into him. It had been a very long time since she'd felt the strength of a man's support. She'd forgotten how sharing a burden could lighten the load. She smiled up at him. Surely between the two of them, they could figure out some way to solve this problem.

At that moment, a familiar black limousine made its way toward them. "That's Carrie," Hannah said softly, dread coursing through her as she thought of the little girl and what her reaction might be when she discovered her beloved Peter was gone.

"I'll go home and come back in an hour," Alex said. "Will you be okay?"

Hannah nodded.

"You don't have to go home," Edna said gruffly. "You can come inside and wait in the kitchen with me. I baked a fresh cherry pie this morning." Edna didn't wait for Alex's reply. She turned and disappeared into the house.

Alex looked at Hannah with a surprised smile. "Is it possible the 'Ice Queen' is warming where I'm concerned?"

Hannah grinned. "I'll give you a small hint. If you want to stay in her good graces, rave about the cherry pie." He laughed, and went into the house.

Taking a deep breath, Hannah went to meet Carrie, who was getting out of the limousine.

Carrie offered a small smile and lifted her hand in greeting as Hannah approached. Again, Hannah felt the cold gnaw of despair in the bottom of her stomach. Carrie was so close, on the verge of a breakthrough, and Hannah feared that the absence of Peter Rabbit might be traumatic enough to thrust the little girl back into her world of total isolation.

"Hi, Carrie," Hannah greeted her. "You look really pretty today. I like your bows in your pigtails."

Carrie reached up and touched one of the red ribbons in acknowledgment, then her gaze darted over toward the rabbit hutch.

"Carrie, let's go over to the front porch and sit down. I need to talk to you."

Carrie cast one more longing look toward the hutch, then followed Hannah to the front porch, where they both sat down.

"Honey, I know you're anxious to go over there and see Peter, but we have a small problem." Hannah hesitated a moment then continued. "It seems somebody opened the door to the hutch and Peter decided to take a little walk. We've looked everywhere for him, but we can't find him."

Carrie's eyes widened, first in disbelief, then in horror. Before Hannah realized the little girl's intentions, Carrie sprang up off the porch and ran toward the hutch. Hannah hurried after her.

When Carrie got to the hutch, she laced her little fingers through the wire and began a keening noise that pierced through Hannah's heart.

"Carrie, honey. I'm sure Peter's fine," Hannah said, pulling the little girl into her arms. "He's just not ready to come home yet."

The keening noise got louder as the little girl burrowed her head in Hannah's shoulder. "I want Peter."

For a moment, Hannah wondered if she'd only imagined the voice, so pitiful and small. "What did you say?" she asked, patting her on the back.

"I want Peter," Carrie repeated, and she burst into tears.

Euphoria flooded Hannah as she realized Carrie was talking. She held the little girl close, listening to her crying, first that she wanted Peter, then that she wanted her mommy. Hannah let her cry, knowing the tears were cathartic, necessary. What she had feared would be a tragedy, had ended up being the catalyst and had caused the ultimate breakthrough for the little girl. Hannah sat down on the grass, pulling Carrie into her lap. As the little girl cried, Hannah rocked her softly. Once the tears were finished, they would have work to do. But for now, the tears were enough.

Alex stared out the window, watching Hannah rocking the child. He felt a curious clutching at his heart, a strange feeling that he'd never experienced before. It wasn't really a pain, yet it made him feel weak in the knees, unable to speak as his throat closed up. For a moment he wondered if he was having a heart attack, but he immediately dismissed the idea. Didn't heart attacks hurt? No, it was seeing Hannah, giving so much of herself, comforting a child in pain that was causing the unusual fullness in his chest.

She would make some mother, he mused. No child of hers would ever doubt her love. No child of hers would ever be less than top priority in her life.

For the first time ever, Alex wondered what it would be like to have a child. Always before, the idea of a wife and family had been some abstract notion in his head. He'd realized eventually he'd marry, probably have a family. But now he found himself contemplating the idea more concretely, surprised to discover it was not an unpleasant thought.

"Here you are—a nice hot cup of coffee and a piece of pie." Edna spoke from behind him.

"She's a special lady, isn't she?" he said, not moving from his vantage point at the window.

Edna joined him there, also staring out to where Hannah sat on the ground. "She's the best. She's been through a lot." She handed him the pie and the cup of coffee, gesturing for him to sit down on the sofa. She sat down in the chair across from him. "I started working for Edward and Hannah two weeks after they got married. I watched Hannah change from a happy, vibrant bride to a disillusioned, miserable young woman. It's taken her a long time to get her self-respect back, find happiness again." She looked at the wall thoughtfully. "Cancer women—they're a strange breed. Hannah can be moody and changeable, but she's also sensitive and sentimental. She's easily hurt and when she loves, it's usually forever." She eyed him critically. "I hope nothing ever happens to shake the self-respect and happiness she's found."

Alex knew the older woman was warning him, and he wasn't sure how to respond. "It's not my intention to hurt Hannah," he finally said.

She eyed him for a long moment, then nodded, as if satisfied by his answer. "You've got to think of something to help her with this neighbor thing. She talked this morning about moving."

"Moving?" Alex wrinkled his brow at the thought.

"She talked about upstate New York or Connecticut." Edna grimaced. "I don't want to move. I've put my roots down here and I'm too old to be transplanted."

Alex placed the piece of pie on the coffee table, his appetite suddenly gone. He walked back over to the window, his mind whirling, trying to come up with some sort of solution to Hannah's problem. As he stared out, a flash of white caught his attention. It was such a quick flash, appearing, then disappearing beneath a large rosebush. For a moment, he thought it was a figment of his imagination, then he realized what it was—a bunny.

"I'll be right back," he said to Edna as he flew out the front door.

He raced to the bush, aware of Hannah and Carrie's curious gazes on him. He got down on his hands and knees, peering into the bush. "Here, little rabbit," he said, reaching into the center and attempting to separate the thorny branches. "Ouch," he exclaimed, stifling a curse as a pointy thorn connected with the back of his hand. "Come out of there, you dumb bunny," he said, moving around to the other side of the bush. At that moment the rabbit flew out from beneath the bush, scampering into the tall grass next to the wooden pen. Alex hurried after him, certain that this was Peter, wanting to get the creature for Carrie and Hannah, who were now standing up and watching his progress.

Alex thundered into the tall grass, standing still as a statue for a moment, waiting for the rabbit to move again. When the grass shuddered to his left, he made a flying dive, winding up with a handful of nothing and scraped knees.

"Alex, move slowly. You're scaring him," Hannah said, smiling at him in encouragement.

He made the okay sign with his fingers, resuming a walk of stealth, moving cautiously forward.

Hannah watched him, stifling a giggle at the incongruous picture he made in his tailored suit and colorful tie, wading through the weeds like a big game hunter stalking a tiger.

"I see him," Alex yelled, and as Hannah and Carrie watched, he dove to the ground once again, disappearing from their sight. There was the sound of him thrashing about as the high grass danced erratically. Then, he reappeared, his tie askew, his hair mussed and a streak of dirt across one cheek. Grinning triumphantly, he held up a fat, fluffy Peter Rabbit. "I got him."

"Peter!" Carrie yelled. And as she ran toward Alex, she did the most amazing thing. Carrie laughed.

* * *

"Edna, this is the best piece of cherry pie I've ever eaten," Alex exclaimed. Carrie had gone home and he sat at the table with Edna and Hannah.

"Oh, go on with you," Edna said, getting up to pour him more coffee.

"No, really. It's definitely the best I've ever had. Maybe you could give the recipe to Jacob."

"I got this recipe from Jacob," she exclaimed, grinning at him knowingly. "But you go ahead and sweet-talk me all you want."

Hannah laughed as a blush decorated Alex's face. She was feeling good. After Alex had found the rabbit, she and Carrie had talked, and Hannah knew the healing process had begun for the little girl.

"Hannah, I've been thinking about your neighbor problem," Alex said, finishing his pie and shoving the plate aside. "I have an idea. I don't know if it will solve anything, but I think it might be a viable plan."

"What is it? I'm willing to try anything."

"Why don't you invite the neighbors here to get to know you, and explain to them what you do here? Let them know that the animals are an important part of your work."

"Oh, I don't know," Hannah replied thoughtfully, finding the idea distressing. "I don't know any of the people around here. I wouldn't even know who to invite."

"I could get a list of names of all the people who live in this immediate area. Like I said, I don't know if it would solve anything, but it might be a beginning."

"It sounds like a good idea to me," Edna said, putting in her two cents' worth. "I could serve coffee and cake. It's hard to be mean to somebody when you've eaten from their table."

"I don't know...." Hannah hesitated, finding the idea of a houseful of hostile neighbors daunting. "I suppose it's not a bad idea...."

"Especially since it's the only one we have," Edna quipped.

"And you wouldn't be facing them alone," Alex continued. "Edna will be here, and so will I." He reached across the table and took her hand in his.

"Okay," Hannah relented, squeezing his hand tightly. "If you get me that list, I'll send out invitations for next Saturday." She offered him a hesitant smile, her stomach still queasy at the thought of facing all those people. Yet, as she felt the warmth of Alex's hand covering hers, saw the caring in his smile, she knew she could face anything if he was at her side.

Chapter Eleven

"Maybe I should have ordered some cold cuts and vegetable trays," Hannah said, worriedly checking the table where two of Edna's special Black Forest cakes were ready to be cut.

"Oh, phooey," Edna scoffed, straightening the cups and saucers stacked on the table. "These people aren't expecting a three-course meal. Your invitation said coffee and cake, so that's what they'll get."

"Do you think this dress is all right? Maybe I should have worn something a little more formal." Hannah smoothed down the skirt of the mint-green sundress, her brow wrinkled with worry.

"You look lovely," Edna exclaimed. "Would you stop fretting? These are your neighbors, not a firing squad. Why don't you go sit down and relax before everyone starts to arrive? And stop fidgeting with your skirt or you'll have it in a dozen wrinkles."

Hannah laced her hands together like an obedient child. She walked over to the window and stared out. The lawn was neatly mowed, the excess grass bagged and carted away. She and Alex had worked throughout the week to make sure the little house and the surrounding area looked neat and orderly for today. It was so important that her neighbors come to accept her, that they accept a truce in this war they had proclaimed. "I wish Alex would hurry up and get here," she said suddenly.

"He promised he'd be here as soon as he could get away from his business meeting," Edna said, reminding Hannah of Alex's phone call an hour earlier.

"I just hope he gets here before anyone arrives," Hannah said faintly, moving away from the window. She wanted Alex at her side. She needed him here with her when the first guests came. He'll be here, she told herself, sitting down on the sofa, careful not to wrinkle the full skirt of her dress. He'll be here because he promised me he would. He knows how important this meeting is to me, how nervous I am about it. He'll be here.

"Maybe we should be serving two kinds of cakes. What if somebody doesn't like Black Forest?" The worried lines were once again back in Hannah's forehead.

"If they don't like my cake, then they aren't normal and we don't want to impress them anyway," Edna exclaimed defiantly. "Why don't you go make a pot of coffee, and keep yourself busy before you drive me crazy with all your worries?''

Smiling apologetically, Hannah moved into the kitchen, where she busied herself making coffee. As the water dripped through the machine, she looked at the clock on the machine. It was nearly time. She'd been hysterical when Alex had called early this morning to tell her he was driving into the city for a business meeting. He'd calmly assured her that he would be back in plenty of time to be here when her neighbors started arriving.

She smiled, leaning against the cabinet as she watched the dark brew fill the glass pot. Alex—in the past week he had been her champion, promising her that this meeting with the neighbors would be fine, that she would show them they had nothing to fear from her or from her animals. More than that, Alex had become her friend. Over the past week she'd come to share with him many of the hopes, the dreams she'd never told anyone else, and he had responded in kind, telling her things she knew he had never shared with anyone.

So, where was he? She had no further time to wonder as at that moment there was a knock on her door.

"Okay?" Edna flashed her a smile of encouragement as she paused momentarily before greeting her guests. Hannah nodded, then taking a deep breath, she opened the door.

"Hello, I'm Marcus Wilkerson, and this is my wife, Marsha." They were an older couple and to Hannah's relief, both wore pleasant smiles.

"Please come in. I'm Hannah Martinof. It was nice of you to come." She led them into the living room where Edna immediately took over the civilities as another knock fell on the door.

Within minutes, the living room was full of people milling about and visiting with each other. In all, there were ten couples, including the parents of the two boys they suspected of doing all the mischief.

When all the people she had invited were there, Hannah knew it was time to tell them exactly why she had invited them here. As she stood before them and called for their attention, she momentarily thought of Alex. She had never needed him more than she did at this moment. He'd promised he'd be here, but his promise wasn't worth the breath he'd used to make it. It was obvious that Alex hadn't thought her fears were important enough to forgo a business meeting. As she faced her neighbors, a piece of her heart turned cold, so cold that she had a feeling it would never be warm again. And Hannah began to talk....

"I certainly didn't understand that you were a psychologist," Marsha Wilkerson spoke up after Hannah had explained exactly what it was she did. "I heard some crazy rumors about animal sacrifices going on here." She shot an angry glare to the parents of the two young boys. "It's amazing how ignorant some people can be."

"I think what you're doing here is quite admirable," Larry Smithers remarked. He pulled a card from his breast pocket. "I'm a lawyer. Please call me if you have any further problems here."

Hannah took his card, grateful that the atmosphere of the gathering seemed to be flowing in her favor. The mood continued to be upbeat as Edna served the cake and coffee. Hannah knew the afternoon was a success, but she didn't feel triumphant. Instead she felt the cold bite of loneliness, the bitter taste of disillusionment. Alex was supposed to have been here to face this with her, share this experience, but as she had done for as long as she could remember, she had handled it all alone, with only Edna's loving support. This might be the beginning of a new relationship with her neighbors, but she knew with a sinking finality that it was also the end of her relationship with Alex.

"Damn," Alex muttered, checking his wristwatch as he zoomed down the parkway. He was late, far later than he'd intended. But it couldn't be helped. The meeting he'd just had and what he'd just accomplished was more important than anything he'd ever done. He patted his shirt pocket, reassured by the crinkling of the papers held within. He was aware that Hannah was probably going to be upset with him for not getting to her place on time, but he was certain she would understand when she realized what he had done.

Hannah... He smiled as he thought of her. Who would have imagined that a crazy sheep would have brought a woman like her into his life? She had brought such joy to him, and he was hoping that the surprise he held in his pocket would bring her an equal amount of happiness.

When he pulled up in front of Hannah's, he was surprised to see there were no other cars there. Apparently the gathering was over. He steeled himself for Hannah's wrath, sure that he would be able to turn her anger into joy.

She answered his knock on the door, and when she saw it was him, she simply turned around and walked back into the living room, leaving him standing just inside the door.

He followed, feeling the arctic air that emanated from her. "Hannah, I'm really sorry I'm late," he began, watching as she gathered up the dirty dishes that were scattered around the room and set them onto a tray.

She shrugged her shoulders, as if it didn't matter.

He watched her for a moment as she worked, waiting for her to say something, *anything,* to him, but there was only silence. "Could you stop that for a moment and talk to me?" he asked, frustrated as she refused to meet his eyes. He'd been expecting anger, recriminations. He had not been expecting this silent cold, like the killing frigid air of a blizzard.

"There's nothing I have to say to you, and nothing you can say that might interest me," she returned, her voice curiously flat. She continued to pile dishes onto the tray.

Alex walked over to her and took her arm, gently turning her around so that he could see her face, look into her eyes. The jeweled green eyes he'd always thought so beautiful, those that had always radiated such emotion, now offered nothing, like a dessert that had lost its flavor, a scent that had faded. "Hannah, please don't be angry. If there was any way I could have gotten here in time, I would have been here." He sighed in frustration as she jerked out of his grasp.

"I understand—you would have been here but your meeting ran late." Her voice was still colorless, like she was commenting on the state of the weather, or a situation far removed from herself. She was obviously much more angry than Alex had anticipated.

"Yes, but Hannah, the meeting I had was for you." He tried to suppress his excitement, anticipating her reaction when he showed her what he had in his pocket.

"For me?" This finally got her full attention. She turned and looked at him. She tried not to notice how achingly handsome he looked. She didn't want to think of how much she loved him. "What sort of meeting could you have that would involve me?"

He grinned, a secret-holding one that made his eyes glow with warmth. Hannah steeled herself against him, trying to summon the anger that had thrummed through her earlier when he hadn't shown up. As she replayed in her mind the moment she'd had to face her neighbors alone, the promise he'd made that had been broken, the anger reappeared, surging through her.

"I met with Edward. Here." He reached into his shirt pocket and withdrew a sheet of paper. "This is for you," he said, handing it to her.

Despite her anger, she took it, curious as to what business he and Edward would have that concerned her. She opened the paper, immediately realizing it was the deed to her house and the surrounding land, the deed that Edward had been holding over her head for years. Bitterness crawled up in her throat as she realized what Alex had done.

She carefully folded the deed and handed it back to him. "When I was growing up, my father never managed to attend any of my birthday parties. Oh, he'd promise, but something would always come up that was more important. Still, he always bought me a wonderfully expensive gift to make up for his absence. Then when I was married to Edward and he missed a party or a gathering that was important to me, he usually bought me a piece of jewelry—a diamond necklace, or a ruby pin." She smiled, the expression holding no joy. "I must be getting better—now I rate real estate." She saw the look of disappointed surprise on his face before she turned back to finish gathering up the dirty dishes.

"Hannah, you don't understand... I bought this land for you... for us. So we wouldn't have to worry about the neighbors forcing Edward to make you move." He walked between her and the coffee table in an attempt to stymie her move away from him. "Hannah, please." He took her arm once again. "I'm sorry I wasn't here, but I thought this business with Edward was more important."

The tight control Hannah had been trying to maintain since the moment he'd arrived, suddenly snapped.

She jerked her arm out of his grasp and faced him, her eyes now blazing with emotion. "More important?" She laughed sarcastically. "Oh, Alex, don't you understand anything? What was important to me was that you promised me you'd be here to support me when I faced those people. You promised you'd be here by my side, and you weren't. Just like my father, just like Edward, you bought me something instead of giving of yourself." Her voice trembled and to her horror she felt tears burning with the need to be released.

She took a deep breath, desperately seeking to regain her control. "I knew from the very beginning that it was foolish for me to try to have a relationship with somebody like you. Edna warned me. She's told me over and over again that Aries and Cancers aren't good for each other. I knew I was flirting with disaster, but like a fool, I hoped." She looked at him, her eyes meeting his sadly. "But now I realize that you're hopeless, Alexander Donaldson, and I don't want to see you anymore."

Alex stared at her wordlessly for a long moment. "You can't mean that," he said in a tone so low she could barely hear him.

It took every ounce of her willpower to face him, look right into his eyes. "I do mean it, Alex."

He flushed slightly and his eyes searched her face as if he was looking for some sign of weakness he could exploit. She raised her chin defiantly, not taking her gaze from his. She knew if she showed him any vulnerability, he would breach through the wall she was trying to erect, a wall that was necessary. She couldn't go through another heartbreak. Edward had been a mere heart palpitation, but Alex had the feel of a full-blown heart attack. She had to get away from it now, before it proved fatal.

"You're a fool, Hannah," he said angrily, throwing the deed down onto the coffee table. "You keep this—it was attained for you." With that, he turned around and stomped out of the house.

Hannah moved over to the window, watching as he got into his car, slammed the door, then roared up the road to his house. "No, Alex, not a fool," she whispered against the windowpane. "I'm a survivor," she finished, just getting the words out before the sobs escaped.

Alex didn't stop at his house, but instead headed his car northeast, toward the point of Long Island. Anger rippled through him, causing him to drive until he could get his emotions under control.

Hannah Martinof. Who needed her? She was crazy, insane. Most women would have been thrilled to be handed the deed to their property. She'd had a problem and he'd worked to solve it in the only way he knew how. What did she want from him? Obviously the question was purely rhetorical now. She wanted nothing from him. She didn't want to see him again. Well, that was fine with him. He'd had enough of the crazy woman with her silly sheep and talk of images in clouds and incompatible astrological signs.

What he needed was to put his efforts back into his business. Since his vacation, since meeting Hannah, he'd slacked off, forgotten how comforting, how safe the world of business could be. It was a world he knew, one where he was comfortable, and it was time to return to it, instead of wasting his energies on a perplexing woman whom he couldn't seem to please. With this thought in mind, he turned his car around and headed back to his office in New York City.

Chapter Twelve

Hannah stood on the front porch, waving as Carrie's limousine carried the little girl away. What progress she was making. Each session Carrie opened up a little bit more. Hannah should have been happy, but that was a word, an emotion she couldn't summon, not since that day two weeks ago when she had ordered Alex out of her life.

She knew she should go inside. Edna would have dinner ready, but she was reluctant to leave the beauty of the evening. Over the past two weeks summer had arrived, bringing with it the scent of flowers in full bloom, the sun-baked smell of the earth, the sound of bugs buzzing and clicking lethargically in the heat of the afternoon. Summer was her favorite season, and yet Hannah could find little pleasure.

How was she to have guessed how empty she would feel without Alex? Despite all her precautions, despite all of her reservations, she'd done the unimaginable and fallen in love with him. Now, all she needed to figure out was how to stop all the feelings that assailed her each time she thought of him.

"Hannah, are you ready to eat?" Edna stepped out onto the porch.

"I'm really not very hungry," Hannah answered, summoning up a smile for the older woman.

"You have to eat," Edna returned. "And you don't have to force a smile for me. I know how you're hurting and I'd like to wring his neck," Edna finished vehemently.

Hannah directed her gaze to the ridge, knowing Alex was just on the other side. "It's really my own fault. You tried to warn me, remember?" She smiled distantly. "You told me I needed to develop Alexphobia." The smile slowly faded. "I was determined not to fall in love with him when we first met, but as we got to know each other, I really thought Alex was different. I thought there was a chance that he might learn to love... maybe I am a fool," she finished with a bitter laugh.

"Never," Edna said, placing an arm around Hannah's shoulders. "Alexander Donaldson is the only fool in these parts. Now, come on and eat, and I'll tell you all the gossip I heard when I was at the stores this afternoon."

Hannah smiled at her gratefully, knowing Edna would keep up a running dialogue that would fill

Hannah's head, and hopefully make thoughts of Alex impossible. Together the two women went inside the house.

Alex sat at his desk, staring out the window into the clouds that formed unusual patterns in the sky. He was vaguely aware of the drone of voices going on around him—his legal department hashing out a problem in the contracts between Wilding Electronics and the Donaldson Corporation.

Hannah's face—why was it that each cloud seemed to hold her image? Why was it that everywhere he looked, in everything he did, she was never far from his mind? He rubbed his forehead as if he could physically banish her from his brain if he rubbed hard enough. Always before, when he'd finished with a woman, it had been easy to forget her, but Hannah was a persistent memory, refusing to be banished.

"I still maintain we need to change the wording of this sentence. It's ambiguous as it stands," Tom Richards exclaimed.

"It's only ambiguous if it's read incorrectly," objected another of the firm's lawyers.

"Alex, what do you think?" Both men turned their attention to him. Alex stared at them both, suddenly too restless to sit still another minute and listen to business talk. He shoved back from his desk and stood up, running his hands tiredly over his face.

"I think I really don't give a damn," he said, causing the two men's faces to blanch in shock. "I'm going home. You all can work out this problem. That's why I pay you an ungodly salary." Without waiting for a response, he walked out of the room.

Maybe he just needed to go home, get some rest. He'd been working fifteen- to twenty-hour days for the past two weeks, fighting the restless frustration that had been a part of his life for as long as he could remember.

He left the office, driving toward his house on Long Island. As he drove, he replayed the past two weeks. He'd managed to close an important deal, one that would prove very lucrative over the next couple of years. He should be feeling terrific, but instead he felt a curious emptiness inside. Even though he had been working so many long hours, he wasn't finding his work satisfying any longer. Instead, it was just a way to get through each day, fill the long hours. Something had changed, he couldn't figure it out and the helplessness of that feeling made him angry. It was like being a hamster on a wheel, moving his legs as fast as possible and getting nowhere. There was only one time in his life that he hadn't felt that curious restlessness, that need to achieve, and that had been with Hannah. This thought only managed to make him angrier, and the anger stayed with him till he got home.

"Jacob," he bellowed as he walked in the front door. "I'm home."

"Good afternoon, sir," Jacob said, appearing in the hallway looking unruffled by his employer's sudden appearance. "Can I get you anything?"

"No...yes. I'd like a Scotch and water." Alex flopped down onto the sofa. He watched as Jacob poured the drink. "Why don't you fill yourself a glass and join me," he said as Jacob handed him the glass. Jacob looked at him in astonishment. "Oh, for goodness' sakes, Jacob, get yourself a drink and sit down."

"Yes, sir."

"And don't call me *sir,*" Alex said irritably, then was immediately contrite as Jacob looked at him in shocked surprise. "I'm sorry, Jacob. I didn't mean to snap at you." Alex sighed and waited until the old man had poured himself a healthy shot of Scotch and sat down on the edge of the chair across from him. "Jacob, what do you know about women?"

Jacob didn't answer for a moment. He took a sip of his Scotch, his brow wrinkled in thought. "I find them a most difficult thing to understand," he finally said. "They seem to view things differently than men, and they tend to get prickly over the smallest things."

"Prickly...that's an understatement." Alex snorted. "Was my father a happy man?" he asked suddenly.

"He was a successful man. He was well-respected in the business world."

"But you didn't answer my question," Alex replied, looking at Jacob curiously.

Again, the older man took a long moment before answering. He smoothed his bushy white eyebrows and took another sip of his drink. "It's hard for me to say. I'm not in a position to discuss another man's feelings. But if I had to guess, I'd say no. Your father was not a happy man." The words came with difficulty to his lips, letting Alex know that Jacob was not a man accustomed to talking about the people who employed him. "Your father was a man searching for something. He thought he could find it in every business deal, every successful merger. But it was never enough." Jacob took another deep drink and eyed Alex critically. "You're a lot like your father." Jacob flushed as Alex stared at him angrily. "I'm sorry, sir, I shouldn't have said that."

The anger Alex had felt momentarily, drained away as he realized Jacob had only spoken what he perceived to be the truth. And wasn't there a certain amount of truth there? A man searching for something, looking for happiness in every business deal, every successful merger, finding that no amount of success could assuage the emptiness, the loneliness that ate at his soul. He'd found the answer once, in Hannah, and he'd blown it, not understanding that the very thing he was beginning to realize was the same thing she'd been trying to teach him.

Cycles. Hadn't Hannah once said something about the endless cycles of unhappiness? Children behaving like parents, living what they're taught. Alex thought of his father, a cold, cheerless man who'd seen everything in life as it related to money and success. Did he really want to pattern his life after his father's? No. What he wanted was Hannah. This thought came out of the blue, fanning the flame of frustration that had been subtly stewing for the past two weeks.

"I can't figure out what that woman wants," he suddenly said.

"I presume we're now talking about Ms. Martinof," Jacob said, pouring himself some more Scotch from the bottle on the table.

Alex got up off the sofa and walked over to the window, staring out toward the ridge that separated his property from Hannah's. "Did you know I bought that land from Edward Martinof and tried to give the deed to Hannah? She didn't want it, was offended by it." Alex turned back around to face Jacob. "Any of the other women I dated would have been thrilled at such a gesture."

"Perhaps it's because Hannah is different that you love her," Jacob commented.

"Who said anything about me loving Hannah?" Alex asked indignantly, noting Jacob's use of her first name.

Jacob smiled and finished his second Scotch. "If it looks like a duck, walks like a duck, and quacks like a duck... it's a duck."

Alex stared at Jacob for a long moment, then turned back around and stared out the window once again. In love with Hannah? Yes, there was a rightness about it that instantly filled his soul with joy. He was in love with Hannah, and it suddenly seemed important that he tell her. "Jacob, you're a genius," Alex exclaimed, turning around to look at the older man. Alex grinned. Jacob was apparently unaccustomed to drinking two glasses of good Scotch, for he was sound asleep, still looking as proper as ever except for the puffy little snores that escaped his lips.

Grabbing an afghan, Alex covered the sleeping man, then headed for the back door. He'd run to Hannah's. He felt much too alive to drive. He wanted to greet her with the smell of sunshine in his hair, the pleasure of life in his eyes.

It wasn't until he reached her place and was ready to knock on her door that doubts worked their way into his mind. What if she didn't want to listen to him? What if she didn't give him a chance to tell her what he needed to say? He straightened his shoulders. He had to tell her. Even if she said it was too late, even if she said it didn't matter, he had to tell her he loved her. He knocked loudly.

"What are you doing here?" Edna glared at him when she opened the door.

"I need to talk to Hannah."

"She doesn't want to talk to you."

"Edna, please," he said with unaccustomed humility.

"It's all right, Edna." Hannah appeared next to the housekeeper. "What do you want?" She tried to still the way her heart jumped erratically at the sight of him.

"We need to talk," he replied, and before she could protest, he took her hand and pulled her out of the door.

He led her to the grassy area beneath a large tree, the same spot where they'd had their first session when he'd pretended to suffer from arachnophobia. "Sit down," he ordered her.

She balked, staring up at him defiantly, recognizing the aggression that lined his face, the ruthless light in his eyes. Hannah glanced over at the pen, reassured to see Sherman there. At least Alex wasn't here to complain about the sheep's misdeeds.

"Please, Hannah." He softened his tone. "Please sit down and listen to what I have to say."

Hannah sat down on the grass and watched as he began to pace back and forth in front of her. Oh, why did he have to look so gorgeous in his tailored business suit? Why did just the mere sight of him have to bring up all the memories of what they had shared, all the heartache of what could never be?

"I'm not even sure where to begin," he said, running a hand over his face, pausing to press his forehead as if to rid himself of a headache. He stopped pacing and turned to her. The aggression and ruthlessness she'd seen were gone; only uncertainty and open vulnerability were left behind.

"You are the most perplexing woman I have ever met. You are also the most beautiful, the most giving and the most desirable—"

"Alex . . ." She wanted him to stop. Was he here because he'd decided he wanted to continue seeing her? To him it might be a challenge, a game, but to her it was too painful to contemplate.

"Please, let me finish," Alex continued. He took up pacing once again. "From the very beginning, I've tried to figure out how to get to you, how to attain access into that secret part of yourself that you hold back. I tried seduction, I tried persuasion. Maybe someplace deep inside I even tried to buy you by getting this property from Edward and giving you the deed." He crouched down next to her and took her hand in his. "Hannah, I want you in my life. Not as a neighborhood psychologist, not as a friend just over the ridge. I want you in my life on a permanent basis. I need you with me every day, in my bed every night." His eyes were compelling, warm and golden, but Hannah was surprised to recognize a sort of desperate humbleness there, as well.

"Hannah, I know I've made mistakes, and to be perfectly honest, I'll probably continue to do so. I need you to remind me what's really important in life. I need you to help me remember the priorities."

"Alex . . . I'm not sure what you're asking of me." Was he asking her to be his mistress? The thought was an ache piercing through her heart.

"Honey—" he squeezed her fingertips "—I want you to marry me, and the only thing I have left to offer you is my love."

Hannah blinked rapidly several times, trying to orient herself to exactly what he was saying. Marriage to Alex? Dare she take a chance? He'd already proven to her that he didn't always make the right choices, that old habits die hard. But hadn't he shown her another side, as well? She thought of the day the animals had been let loose, how he had dropped everything and come to help. She could still picture him in her mind, dressed in his business suit, beating the bushes for a missing rabbit. Yes, he had made some bad choices, but he'd made some good ones, too.

"I don't know much about this star stuff, but surely there are other Arians and Cancerians who make a go at a relationship. Surely we can overcome whatever obstacles the stars put in our way. Hannah, I love you." There was such longing, such blatant emotion on his face, in his voice, that she could do nothing but believe him.

"Oh, Alex." Her voice caught on a sob and she threw herself into his arms. "That's all I want, that's all I need, is to know you love me." Her body was warm and pliant against his. "Yes, Alex, yes, I'll marry you."

He cupped her face in his hands and gazed at her with such tenderness that had she had any doubts about her decision, they would have been swept away. "I love you, Hannah," he repeated in a whisper and his lips claimed hers hungrily. "These past two weeks without you have been hell," he said as they broke the kiss. He smiled down at her. "You know it won't be easy. We'll have to come up with some compromises. I can't promise that I won't mess up again, make a bad decision."

"I can see I have my work cut out for me," she said with a smile. "I'm just going to have to prove to you that it's much more fun to spend time in the bedroom instead of in a boardroom."

His eyes glittered brightly, then he frowned again. "Yes, but..."

"Shh." She laid a finger against his lips. "We'll make it, Alex. And just remember if you do make a bad decision, I'm not the only one you'll have to face."

"What do you mean?" He looked at her curiously.

She smiled and motioned toward the house where Edna stood twisting a dish towel, looking as if she were fashioning it into a lethal weapon.

They both laughed, and in the sound of her laughter, the love in her eyes, Alex discovered the true meaning of wealth and success.

Epilogue

"Breathe, honey, come on." Edna puffed along with Hannah until the contraction had passed, then she took a cloth and gently swiped it across Hannah's forehead.

"Mrs. Donaldson, we really need to get you into the delivery room immediately," the nurse said with a brisk smile.

"No, not yet," Hannah protested with a gasp. "I'm waiting for my husband."

"I'll go check with Jacob and see if he's heard anything from Alex." Edna patted Hannah's arm and left the labor room.

Hannah closed her eyes, preparing herself for the next contraction. She focused her thoughts on Edna and Jacob, a smile touching her lips. In the year since

Hannah's marriage to Alex, Edna and Jacob had continued their unusual courtship, arguing about how the big house should be run, then making up with coy smiles and fond gazes. Hannah had a feeling it wouldn't be long before wedding bells would chime for them.

It was hard for her to believe that she and Alex had been married an entire year. Each day had breezed by on wings of love and laughter. Her little carriage house had become her office, and she and Alex escaped there on weekends when they didn't want to be disturbed. She smiled. She had a feeling it had been one of those very cozy weekends that had gotten her into this present condition.

"There's no sign of him yet," Edna said, coming back into the room. "Hannah, honey, maybe he really couldn't get away from the meeting. Maybe you should let them go ahead and take you into the delivery room."

"No, he'll be here and I'm not going to have this baby until he is," Hannah replied with a note of stubbornness.

The nurse laughed. "Mrs. Donaldson, I'm afraid you aren't in control in this particular situation. You've got a baby who's most anxious to be born."

"Well, he's just going to have to wait for his father."

At that moment Alex flew through the door, his eyes wild with anxiety. "Oh, thank God, I was afraid I'd be too late."

"Where have you been? We've all been waiting for you," Edna exclaimed impatiently, but her eyes sparked with fondness.

"I had to stop and pick up something I had made for the baby." He leaned over and kissed Hannah on the forehead. "Then when I got it, it wouldn't fit into my car, so I had to flag down a taxi."

"I should have known you stopped to buy something," Hannah exclaimed, giggling at his stricken expression, then assuring him, "It's all right. What on earth did you get?" She managed to say it just before she began her breathing exercise again.

With a huge grin, Alex stepped out of the room, then reappeared, carrying the largest stuffed animal Hannah had ever seen. When he set it on the floor, she realized it was a woolly sheep with pink and blue ribbons tied around its neck.

"Oh, Alex...he's going to love it." Hannah laughed with a pant as another contraction began.

"Yes, *she* will," he agreed with a grin. It had been an ongoing argument. She wanted a little boy with golden brown eyes and he wanted a little girl with big green eyes. He leaned over Hannah and kissed her gently. "I figured our baby needed her very own sheep. After all, look what Sherman did for us. He knew all along we were right for each other."

"Alex, would you do me a favor?" Hannah asked, biting down on her bottom lip.

"Anything, my love."

"Could you get me into the delivery room? I'm going to have this baby right now."

* * *

Several hours later, Hannah lay in her hospital room, Alexander Donaldson IV snuggled in the crook of her arm. Alex, who had been with her in the delivery room, had said very little since seeing the birth of his son.

"Alex, are you okay?" She looked at him worriedly. "I mean, you don't mind, do you? That he's a boy?"

Alex shook his head. "No, it's not that...." He took her hand, a curious expression on his face. "I just never knew..." he began, his voice thick with awe. "I never dreamed..."

Hannah smiled. "I know, it's a miracle, isn't it?" She reached out and ran her hand down the side of his face. "I love you, Alex."

"That's the first miracle in my life."

"And now I have another Aries man in my life to love," she said, smiling down at the infant in her arms.

"He's the second miracle in my life." As Alex leaned over to kiss his wife and newborn son, he felt fulfilled, complete. And he was grateful that he'd finally discovered the key to Hannah—love.

* * * * *

LOVE AND
THE ARIES MAN

by Wendy Corsi

In spring, a young man's fancy turns to thoughts of love . . . and the passionate Aries man is no exception. His boundless energy and daring allow him to pursue his heart's desire with unrivaled persistence. Once he's set his cap for an unsuspecting woman, her romantic destiny has been decided. And if she tries to play hard to get, he'll be all the more intrigued—this die-hard Romeo thrives on challenge! But the woman he chooses couldn't be luckier, for the Aries man makes a sincere, generous, loving husband . . . and his eternal optimism will smooth any rough spots on their marital path.

WHATEVER ALEX WANTS . . . Alex gets! When aggressive Aries Alexander Donaldson III sets out to woo reluctant Hannah Martinof, wedding bells weren't far off. But first he had a thing or two to learn about finding time to appreciate everyday beauty with his nature-loving Cancer woman. What can you teach the Aries man about life . . . and love?

When two ambitious *Arians* make a permanent commitment, they're apt to achieve their lifelong marital goals in the first year! But these two are so alike they'll inevitably lock horns over countless issues—for starters, who gets to be boss. Hopefully the Aries man will quickly learn that he's met his match, and realize a little compromise can go a long way toward household harmony!

The Aries man makes quick decisions, and he'll immediately recognize that the loyal *Taurus* woman would be an ideal mate. But he'll have to be patient while she makes up her mind about him! Yet once she's his, she's his, forever. The Aries man should take a lesson from the cautious Taurus and resolve not to go tearing through life anymore—it's worth slowing down to keep his careful, sensible woman by his side!

There are few challenges an Aries man can't conquer—but a **Gemini** woman might be one of them. This elusive charmer will keep the smitten Aries man guessing, and just when he thinks he's figured her out, she'll do an about-face. She's smart and subtle, and a few sharp battles of wits with her will teach the occasionally arrogant Aries man not to underestimate his mate!

The stylish *Leo* woman always looks great, so who can blame the appreciative Aries man for falling head over heels in love at first sight? This fiery match will blaze beyond surface chemistry, with plenty of sparring and passionate reconciliations. Though they both hate to lose arguments, the Leo lady will occasionally give in for his sake. Never one to be shown up, the Aries man may take her lead and gradually learn to soften his own edges!

It won't be easy for the reserved, organized *Virgo* woman to adjust to her Aries mate's hyperactivity, but she's willing to learn for the sake of true love. In turn, he'll strive to convince this ladylike treasure that he's deserving of her favors. With her calm guidance, he'll rein in his chaotic impulses—but never enough to make life lose its sparkle!

The peaceful *Libra* woman is probably somewhat baffled by the Aries man's rampant risk-taking. But she knows his forward-looking philosophy is the perfect complement to her old-fashioned sentimentality, and she values this balance in her life. Eventually her romantic streak may rub off on the Aries man, and they'll **both** be surprised when he takes to whispering sweet nothings in his beloved's ear!

The secretive *Scorpio* woman is sure to attract the enigma-seeking Aries man. He'll find her sexy and supportive, and when it comes to stamina, she'll give him a run for his money. As their relationship deepens, the usually restless Aries man will probably be less caught up in worldly ventures...and more intrigued by the fascinating woman at home!

When an Aries man teams up with a *Sagittarius* woman, one thing is certain—he's in for tons of fun!

These two fire signs understand each other well, which makes for a minimum of conflict when it comes to daily issues like housework and socializing. If they're both lucky, the Sagittarius woman's positive influence may even combat the Aries man's tendency to lapse into self-centeredness!

With a dedicated *Capricorn* woman standing beside him, the Aries man will feel capable of achieving his loftiest goals—and for him, few things are more important. He might be tempted to take this traditional, faithful female for granted, but she's full of surprises. By revealing her hidden passionate nature at just the right moments, she'll teach the Aries man that still waters run deep....

The Aries man can't help but admire the altruistic *Aquarius* woman's ambitious purpose in life—to make the world a better place. But she doesn't count on him when it comes to pursuing her more unconventional interests—he's busy with his own activities, and this diversity will keep them both fascinated. If he's willing, she'll be able to broaden his horizons considerably.

The *Pisces* woman is a romantic dreamer, and she'll be captivated by the Aries man's masculine daring. He'll be fascinated by her changing moods—from frilly little-girl coyness to sleek sexiness.... This woman will dazzle him daily! But he'll have to remember that for all her unpredictability, she's **always** emotional—and he should never forget to treat her gently.

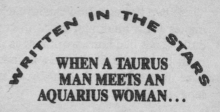

SILHOUETTE® *Desire*™

FREE GIFT OFFER

To receive your free gift, send us the specified number of proofs-of-purchase from any specially marked Free Gift Offer Harlequin or Silhouette book with the Free Gift Certificate properly completed, plus a check or money order (do not send cash) to cover postage and handling payable to Harlequin/Silhouette Free Gift Promotion Offer. We will send you the specified gift.

FREE GIFT CERTIFICATE

ITEM	A. GOLD TONE EARRINGS	B. GOLD TONE BRACELET	C. GOLD TONE NECKLACE
# of proofs-of-purchase required	3	6	9
Postage and Handling	$1.75	$2.25	$2.75
Check one	☐	☐	☐

Name: _____

Address: _____

City: _____ State: _____ Zip Code: _____

Mail this certificate, specified number of proofs-of-purchase and a check or money order for postage and handling to: HARLEQUIN/SILHOUETTE FREE GIFT OFFER 1992, P.O. Box 9057, Buffalo, NY 14269-9057. Requests must be received by July 31, 1992.

PLUS—Every time you submit a completed certificate with the correct number of proofs-of-purchase, you are automatically entered in our MILLION DOLLAR SWEEPSTAKES! No purchase or obligation necessary to enter. See below for alternate means of entry and how to obtain complete sweepstakes rules.

MILLION DOLLAR SWEEPSTAKES
NO PURCHASE OR OBLIGATION NECESSARY TO ENTER

To enter, hand-print (mechanical reproductions are not acceptable) your name and address on a 3"×5" card and mail to Million Dollar Sweepstakes 6097, c/o either P.O. Box 9056, Buffalo, NY 14269-9056 or P.O. Box 621, Fort Erie, Ontario L2A 5X3. Limit: one entry per envelope. Entries must be sent via 1st-class mail. For eligibility, entries must be received no later than March 31, 1994. No liability is assumed for printing errors, lost, late or misdirected entries.

Sweepstakes is open to persons 18 years of age or older. All applicable laws and regulations apply. Sweepstakes offer void wherever prohibited by law. Prizewinners will be determined no later than May 1994. Chances of winning are determined by the number of entries distributed and received. For a copy of the Official Rules governing this sweepstakes offer, send a self-addressed, stamped envelope (WA residents need not affix return postage) to: Million Dollar Sweepstakes Rules, P.O. Box 4733, Blair, NE 68009.

SR1U

ONE PROOF-OF-PURCHASE
To collect your fabulous FREE GIFT you must include the necessary FREE GIFT proofs-of-purchase with a properly completed offer certificate.

(See center insert for details)